OTHER NOVELS BY PHYLLIS SHALANT

When Pirates Came to Brooklyn

Bartleby of the Mighty Mississippi

The Great Eye

Beware of Kissing Lizard Lips

BARTLEBY of the
Big Bad Bayou

BARTLEBY
of the
Big Bad Bayou

PHYLLIS SHALANT

with illustrations by **BRIAN FLOCA**

DUTTON CHILDREN'S BOOKS · NEW YORK

DUTTON CHILDREN'S BOOKS
A division of Penguin Young Readers Group
Published by the Penguin Group
Penguin Group (USA) Inc., 375 Hudson Street, New York, New York 10014, U.S.A.
Penguin Group (Canada), 10 Alcorn Avenue, Toronto, Ontario, Canada
M4V 3B2 (a division of Pearson Penguin Canada Inc.)
Penguin Books Ltd, 80 Strand, London WC2R 0RL, England
Penguin Ireland, 25 St Stephen's Green, Dublin 2, Ireland (a division of Penguin Books Ltd)
Penguin Group (Australia), 250 Camberwell Road, Camberwell, Victoria 3124,
Australia (a division of Pearson Australia Group Pty Ltd)
Penguin Books India Pvt Ltd, 11 Community Centre, Panchsheel Park,
New Delhi - 110 017, India
Penguin Group (NZ), Cnr Airborne and Rosedale Roads, Albany, Auckland 1310,
New Zealand (a division of Pearson New Zealand Ltd)
Penguin Books (South Africa) (Pty) Ltd, 24 Sturdee Avenue, Rosebank,
Johannesburg 2196, South Africa
Penguin Books Ltd, Registered Offices: 80 Strand, London WC2R 0RL, England

Library of Congress Cataloging-in-Publication Data
Shalant, Phyllis.
Bartleby of the big bad bayou / Phyllis Shalant.
p. cm.
Summary: After making a dangerous voyage down the Mississippi from
New York, Bartleby, who had started life as a pet turtle, and his alligator friend
Seezer must learn to survive in their true bayou home.
ISBN 0-525-47366-1 (alk. paper)
1. Turtles—Juvenile fiction. [1. Turtles—Fiction. 2. Bayous—Fiction.
3. Animals—Fiction.] I. Title.
PZ10.3.S38425Bar 2005   [Fic]—dc22   2004022232

Published in the United States by Dutton Children's Books,
a division of Penguin Young Readers Group
345 Hudson Street, New York, New York 10014
www.penguin.com/youngreaders

Designed by Gloria Cheng

Printed in USA   First Edition
1 3 5 7 9 10 8 6 4 2

For Beverly,
who accidentally fried our goldfish
on the radiator, whose hamster escaped
in our bedroom, and who once
wanted an iguana

Bartleby

THE SWAMP

OLD STUMP'S BAYOU

THE WOODS

THE LEVEE

← TO CHEF JERRY'S

THE ROCKY LEDGE

Seezer

Lucky Gal

FRIENDSHIP HOLE

THE MIGHTY MISSISSIPPI

Old Stump

Contents

PART One

Free Lunch

1

Bartleby was crawling along the bank of the wide, rolling water when something caught his eye. It was the glint of crinkly silver stuff lying on the shore. He perked up his head and listened for human voices. He felt the ground under his webs for the vibrations of human footsteps. There didn't seem to be any, so he plodded over to investigate.

Usually there was food inside a silvery wad like this. Not juicy worms or gooey slugs, but human food. A lot of it tasted sweet, which Bartleby detested. But sometimes there was lettuce.

Once Bartleby had been a pet. He'd lived in a house with three boys and a mother. Mostly, they'd fed him turtle flakes. But sometimes, for a special treat, the mother had given him lettuce. Just the thought of it made his mouth tingle happily. He crawled up to the crumpled silver and stuck his head inside.

3

Sure enough, it was there—a crisp-looking leaf poking out from two pieces of the soft, bland food humans sometimes tossed to ducks. Only a few bites were missing. And on top of the lettuce were two slices of something the pinkish brown color of earthworms. It had a spicy smell that Bartleby found interesting. But first he would eat the lettuce. *Snap!* He clamped his jaws down on the tasty green and began to drag it to the river.

"Bartleby, are you sssunning on the bank?" a gruff voice called.

"I'm over here, Seezer! I have found something very delicious. Lettuce! And I think there is something that you would like. Come and try it!"

A blackish green alligator climbed out of the water. Part of his tail was missing. He swung his big head from side to side, scanning the shore, the brush, and the woods beyond. Cautiously, he treaded over the mud bank where Bartleby was waiting.

"Bologna!" he exclaimed, peering into the silvery bundle. "I haven't had bologna since I was a pet. My girl used to ssslip it out of her sssandwich and feed it to me when her mother wasn't looking. Bologna is beautiful ssstuff!"

"You can have it," Bartleby said. "I'll eat the lettuce. There's more than enough."

With a quick clap of his long jaws, Seezer swallowed both pieces of the spicy meat. "Ahhh, ssscrumptious!" He looked around the bank and toward the woods. "But where there is bologna, there are humans. We mustn't ssstay long. Besides, I believe we have finally reached our destination."

Bartleby's mouth opened. He dropped his leaf. "The Mighty Mississippi?" His heart beat faster. "Really? How can you tell?"

"Sssee how the water has become brown and muddy? Sssoon I think we will ssspot great garfish and juicy ssswamp rabbits. Mmmm . . . even better than bologna."

Bartleby didn't want to eat rabbits—and he hoped the great garfish didn't want to eat him. Seezer had told him that the gar was so big and fierce it ate ducks for breakfast and muskrats for dinner! Thinking of it now made Bartleby shudder in his shell. Still, he couldn't wait to get to Seezer's bayou—a cozy creek filled with fresh water from the river. Many times his friend had told him about the delightful water place he'd lived in before he'd been trapped by a pet seller.

Bartleby had been hatched in a tank. He'd never seen a bayou. But he knew it was his natural home, too, because of a show he'd seen on TV when he'd lived with the boys. It had been called *Turtles of the Mighty Mississippi,* and there'd been red-ears like himself in it. More than anything, he longed to meet those turtles.

He seized the lettuce and turned toward the powerful, churning river again. Once the pond in New York where he'd been dumped had been the biggest water place he'd ever swum in. Then he and Seezer had found a trickle of traveling water in which to begin the journey. At first, the moving water had felt so much colder, Bartleby had wanted to dig down under the mud and stay there. He'd had to get used to swimming with the quick, bouncy current—which was fun until he'd crashed into a rock. But now he was a strong swimmer and a good navigator. He was sure his old friends at the pond would be proud of him.

Day after day, Bartleby and Seezer had paddled along the meandering stream, past green-gold forests, rich brown fields, and the gray or tan structures that meant humans' territory. It was a long journey. They'd started during the hottest part of the year, swum on past the days of falling leaves, and fought their way through the time of snow and ice. Now it was the period of newly budding trees. And all the while, their watery way had grown bigger and faster.

Bartleby took another step toward the river—and heard a rustling in the woods.

Awoooo! something howled.

Ruh-ruhruh-ruh! came the answer.

"Dogs! Into the water ssspeedily!" Seezer hissed, sliding down the muddy bank.

Bartleby couldn't resist taking a small bite of lettuce. Suddenly two humans with fishing branches stepped out of the woods. Their noisy dogs ran toward him. It was too late to get back to the water. Instead, he pulled in his head and limbs.

Warm, smelly breath wafted around his shell. Sharp nails pawed at him. Bartleby held his breath and stayed perfectly still. He tried to pretend he was a rock.

The smaller dog nipped the edge of Bartleby's carapace. *Yaw-yaw-yaw-yaw!* it cried. Which meant, "You're not fooling me."

Grrrruh-grrruh-grrruh, answered the bigger dog. Which meant, "I smell an alligator—and I don't like alligators."

"Champ! Buddy! Y'all quiet down before you scare the fish away," ordered a deep human voice. "Now give me that turtle." A human hand grabbed Bartleby and lifted him up. "I think it's a red-ear, although with its head in, it's tough to tell."

"My granny used to cook turtle soup." This was a different voice, higher and scratchier.

Soup? Inside his shell, Bartleby quivered. Although it had been long ago, he remembered his boys eating something called soup. It looked like steaming water with pieces floating in it. He'd never guessed they'd been pieces of turtle.

The hand around him tightened its grip. "Was your granny's soup any good?"

7

"Tasted about as good as a bowl of bathwater—after you've taken the bath. Granny sure was a bad cook. Haw haw!"

Now the hand swung Bartleby up and down. "Well, this one's still young and puny, anyway. Guess I'll let it go. Besides, I'd much rather have a catfish for supper. C'mon, we're wasting time. Let's fish." The hand carried Bartleby to the river and dropped him in. "Here you go, Gator Bait."

The moment he hit the water, Bartleby dove for the bottom. But the human's insults were still ringing in his head. *Puny! Gator Bait!* He didn't think he was puny at all. He was as large as that big man's hand. And he was strong. He was sure he could outswim a man or a dog.

When he reached the river bottom, Seezer was waiting. "I thought you were right behind me," the alligator said. "But when you didn't enter the water, I feared you had been sssnatched—or ssswallowed."

"The humans around here eat turtles!" Bartleby told him. "They only let me go because they thought I was puny."

"Don't worry. Ssswamp food will help you grow. The red-ears in my bayou were as big as basking ssstones. All the beasts here are great and ssstrong. Now let's hurry. I feel sssure we're almost home." Seezer tucked his legs tightly against his body, swished his tail, and began gliding through the water.

As he paddled behind his friend, Bartleby gazed at the endless bands of trees beyond the banks of the river. According to Seezer, the land around the Mighty Mississippi was filled with little waterways like his. How would they ever discover the right one?

"Seezer, will you really be able to find your bayou in this big place?"

"Sssertainly," the alligator replied. "I will sssee, and sssmell, and sssense my way to the old nest where my brothers and sssisters have been waiting for me."

"But you've been gone a long time. Do you think your relatives will still be there?"

"Sssurely! They'll ssselebrate when I return. Oh, I can just imagine the bellowing, and sssplashing, and wrestling. And the feasting!"

Gator Bait. Once more, the man's words came back to Bartleby. What if Seezer's family wanted to make him part of their feast?

As if he could read his red-eared friend's thoughts, Seezer nudged Bartleby with his shortened tail. "Don't worry. I'll sssee that no harm comes to you. I will tell everyone about our long journey together. Besides, there's plenty for everyone to eat in the bayou. One sssmall turtle would hardly make a sssnack for any of them."

As they traveled, the Mighty Mississippi grew muddier and muddier. It became so thick, Bartleby felt as if he were pushing through it instead of swimming. And it was so murky he could barely make out a thing. He nearly bumped into the biggest catfish he'd ever seen, but the creature only went on sweeping the riverbed with its long whiskery feelers. His heart thudded as he stroked past a scrawny muskrat biting at a piece of fishing line tangled around its tail. And when a great boat with a giant spinning wheel gave a shrill *toot-toot,* Bartleby nearly jumped out of his shell. Still he kept on swimming.

"Sssee over there where the bank ssslopes more sssharply?" Seezer asked. With his flat snout, the alligator pointed toward the steep brown shore. "Sssomething inside me is sssaying to go on land now and sssearch for my bayou. You wait here."

Bartleby peered around the dark water. "No—I want to come with you."

"It's better that you ssstay. I will be ssspeedier on my own. I'll just go a little way and check. Then I'll come back for you." Seezer squinted up at the bank. "Sssee that outcrop of rock over the river? It looks like a sssafe place. You can wait for me there."

Bartleby knew that his friend was right. He badly needed a rest. But a strange pang gnawed at his insides. In the time since they'd begun their journey, he and Seezer had never been separated.

"Don't worry, I'll be back sssoon." Seezer slithered up over the bank the way alligators do when they are trying not to be seen.

"Good luck, friend!" Bartleby crawled onto the rocky ledge that hung over the river. As he settled down on the warm, gray stone, he could hear Seezer calling to him from the tall, marshy grass beyond the bank.

"Bartleby, remember—ssstay put!"

At first, Bartleby had never felt more alone in his life. He pulled tightly into his shell, hoping to look like a lump of mud, or a large stone. But after a while the sun on his carapace felt so pleasant, he just had to bask. He poked his head out and stretched his neck and limbs. As the delicious heat warmed him, he began to sense the muzzy feeling that came before a turtle nap. He was nearly asleep when a voice from the water called to him.

"Cousin, will you help me?"

Bartleby felt a little ping of alarm. Should he answer?

"Please, Cousin, I'm asking for your help."

Very slowly, Bartleby crept to the edge of his stony perch. Far away at the pond in New York, he'd had some wonderful friends. His insides still ached when he thought of grumbly, good-hearted Mudly—a stinkpot turtle—and brave, funny Zip, a spring peeper. The idea of meeting a cousin or any relative here was very tempting.

But he hadn't forgotten Seezer's warning. He looked down at the murky surface of the river. He couldn't see anything. "Who is there?" he asked.

"I've told you, it's a cousin. I've caught a tender young crappie, but I can't finish it on my own. Won't you help me eat this tasty fish?"

Bartleby felt a little burst of joy. He'd yearned to forage and eat with others like himself. "Why don't you bring the fish up onto this rock?" he suggested.

"I can't, Cousin. It's too heavy. Besides, dining underwater is much more pleasant. Come into the river."

It was true that red-ears preferred eating underwater. Still, Bartleby felt hesitant. "I can't see where you are. Would you raise your head above the surface for me?"

For a few moments nothing happened. Then, just

12

below the rock ledge, a long body rolled over and over, churning the water into foam. Next, a head popped out. It was the head of an alligator. But instead of being blackish green like Seezer's, it was mud brown on top and sickish yellow under the chin. Instead of the deep-set eyes on the top of Seezer's head, this alligator's eyes were flat and dull. And when the ugly creature opened its mouth, Bartleby saw two rows of teeth in its upper jaw.

He pulled his head in. "I th-thought you said you w-were a cousin."

The strange alligator nodded its head up and down. "I am. I'm an alligator and you're a turtle. All reptiles are related."

Bartleby considered this. "I do have an alligator friend who is as close as family."

The ugly creature showed all its teeth. "See? Then we are family, too."

Bartleby poked his head out to peer at the creature again. "But what a pale underside you have."

"All the better to camouflage myself underwater, Cousin."

"But what flat, fishy eyes you have."

"All the better to see in the dark, muddy deep, Cousin. Now come into the water."

"But what a lot of teeth you have—twice as many in your upper jaw as my alligator friend."

"Listen!" the strange, long-jawed head said sharply. "You have an alligator pal who is like family to you. I am an alligator, and all alligators are first cousins. Therefore, you and I are cousins, too. Now come into the water and we will get properly acquainted. I am growing tired of waiting."

Without a word, the peculiar alligator disappeared underwater. As Bartleby stared at the rings of ripples it left behind, the creature suddenly came crashing up through the surface again. It was aiming right for him with its mouth wide open!

Quickly, Bartleby backed away from the edge of the rock. The alligator thing snapped its jaws greedily, but it couldn't reach him. Before it fell back down into the water, Bartleby caught a glimpse of something strange behind its head. It was a long, narrow body with fish fins and a fishtail at the end.

"You aren't an alligator at all!" he cried. "You're a fish!"

"Don't be silly. If I were a fish, I couldn't breathe air." The ugly head popped up again. It opened its mouth and took a few grunting breaths. "See?"

Bartleby wasn't convinced. "You don't look like the alligator I know. I think you're a faker—a big fish faker."

"I may be a faker, but you're a liar," the alligator-headed fish snarled. "Red-eared turtles do not have alli-gator friends. Red-ears are food for alligators—and for alligator garfishes like me."

"My friend Seezer is nothing like you," Bartleby retorted. "He doesn't eat turtles!"

"Well, I'll just wait here and see. Perhaps when your friend comes back, he and I will share you for lunch." The ghastly gar opened its jaws once more and displayed its horrible choppers.

"Yes, I'm all ssset for lunch. And it is looking quite ssscrumptious!" came a voice from behind Bartleby.

"Seezer, you're back!" Bartleby cried as his friend dove off the rock shelf into the river. In the water below, he saw Seezer's tail thrash. He heard toothy jaws clash. He felt the water splash and splash. Then everything grew still.

Bartleby eyed the dark, quiet surface. Had the giant gar eaten Seezer before they'd even found his bayou? He felt a deep ache above his plastron as he kept watch. The slow, brown river just kept flowing without any sign of his friend.

He'd nearly given up all hope when a great wave blew up from the water and splashed over his carapace. "Ho, what a sssensational ssscuffle!" Seezer bellowed as he shot up through the surface. "The alligator gar is an enemy worth having. Thank you for keeping it busy until I got here."

Bartleby swallowed. "You're welcome. Wh-what happened to it?"

"I'm afraid it escaped. But now that we've reached

bayou country, I'll be able to sssharpen my hunting ssskills. The prey here is delightfully dangerous." Seezer smacked the water with his tail. "Now I have sssweet news. I believe my bayou is through the grass, on the other ssside of the levee, and just beyond the woods. Let's go."

Homecoming Day

3

Bartleby followed Seezer through the sharp-edged grass and over the wide, earthy ridge called a levee. Soon the friends came to the brink of a great, dark wood. Trees like silent giants threw shadows over the land. They spread out their branches like great human arms and trailed long, silvery strands from their fingers.

Bartleby's throat began to pulse. "Giant spiders must live in these trees. Those webs almost reach to the ground."

"Ho, no!" Seezer flicked his tail up and caught a few strings of the gray, mossy material. "I remember this plant well. My sssweet mother ssstuffed our nest with it to make us ssspecially comfy. It marks this land as bayou country. We are almost home. I am sssure of it."

It was a difficult crawl through the tangled floor of the woods. Grasses, ferns, mosses, vines, berry bushes, and ivy covered every bit of ground. But as Bartleby pressed his way deeper into the heart of the place that was his true home, something inside him began to awaken. In a pile of dead leaves, his webs sensed the vibrations of a snake that was hiding, and he plodded away as fast as he could. When he came upon a patch of pointy, yellow-green shoots poking up from the forest floor, he knew before he bit into one that it would be tender and good to eat. He even thought he recognized the bitter-sweet scent of bayou water ahead, although he couldn't see it.

Without warning, they came upon a slow, quiet stream that was carpeted with tiny green leaves and dotted with yellow flowers. All along the banks, trees dipped their branches into the bayou as if they were reaching for a cool drink. It was the most beautiful water place Bartleby had ever seen. Yet it was strangely still. Although he listened, he didn't hear birds calling in the trees or squirrels skittering through the brush. Even the air seemed to be without flies or mosquitoes.

"Is this our bayou?" Bartleby whispered.

"Sssweet Ssswampland, this is it!" Seezer's black eyes sparkled.

"Then where is your family?"

"Bayou creatures are ssshy and careful. But they will sssurely appear when they learn who I am."

Bartleby was eager to try the bayou water. But he also felt a bit wary. He didn't want to run into another gruesome gar. "That blanket of green covering the surface is a good place for hiding in."

Seezer snorted. "No one here would ssseek to harm me. Climb on my back and we'll take our first bayou ssswim together."

Bartleby pulled himself onto his friend's rough hide. Together they slid into the water. It was soft and slick against Bartleby's webs, and warm in just the right way.

"Ahhhh." Seezer sank down deeper. He raised his head and tail, sucking in a big breath of bayou air. "Sssisters, brothers, it is me, Ssseezer," he bellowed. "I'm home! Won't you come and sssay hello to your long-lost relative?"

"That depends. Are you going to share your lunch, bro'?" a voice asked.

Seezer whirled around so fast, Bartleby had to dig his nails in to keep from flying off. Suddenly they were snout to snout with another alligator.

"Sssalutations—are you my brother?" Seezer asked.

The gator gazed at Bartleby with its mouth hanging open. It was so skinny Bartleby could practically see its ribs. "I could be your bro'—if you're willing to share that meal on your back. We could scarf him down together," the scrawny creature answered.

"I am thankful to meet sssome kin at last," Seezer replied. "But this red-ear is no sssnack. He is my friend, Bartleby."

The other alligator eyed Seezer. "Well, a friend wouldn't want you to go hungry, would he? I'm sure he won't mind filling our bellies, bro'."

Bartleby snapped into his shell. It seemed like the creatures here had a funny way of being friends.

"Sssorry. Where I come from, we don't ssswallow friends." Seezer began paddling away.

But the hungry creature followed after him. "I thought you said this bayou was your home, bro'."

Seezer flicked his tail back and forth. "It is true that I was born here. But I was only a youngster when I was caught in a sssnare and sssent all the way to New York. There I ssstayed in a tank until a human dumped me in a pond. Bartleby and I ssswam back here together."

The other alligator slapped his tail against the water. "Woo-hoo, bro'—I've never heard of New York. But it sounds far away! Now let me see—" He glided back and forth, inspecting Seezer from one end to another. "Beautiful, jagged teeth like mine . . . cute little sneaky eyes like mine . . . big tough scutes like mine . . . and—what happened to your tail?"

"I lost sssome of it in a sssscuffle. But there's ssstill enough left to ssstave off enemies." Seezer whipped his tail back and forth to prove it.

His friend hadn't exactly told the truth, Bartleby knew. Seezer's tail had been run over by the wheels of a truck while he was helping Bartleby cross a great road. The memory gave the red-ear a pain above his plastron.

"That sure must have been some fight, bro'. But if you weren't missing the tip of your tail, we'd be the same size—which could mean we're the same age. We might even be from the same clutch of eggs." The gator bumped up against Seezer's side in a friendly way. "Welcome home, bro'. Mama named me Grub because I like to eat and I like to dig."

"Sssweet Ssswampland—so do I! Mama always sssaid digging runs in our family." Seezer swung his head back and forth, gazing from shore to shore. "Where is Mama? Where are our other sssiblings?"

Grub sank down lower in the water. His black eyes lost their shine. "They've all gone. I'm afraid I'm the only one left here."

Seezer clapped his jaws together. "No Mama? No sssiblings? Why would they leave our home? Ours was the sssweetest in all of bayou country."

"It was getting crowded. Chow was becoming scarce."

"But I remember the fish practically ssspringing into our jaws," Seezer protested. "Besides, the members of our family were the most ssskilled hunters and fishers of all. We always had food to sssspare." For a moment he closed his eyes. Bartleby could feel him trembling. Silently, the red-ear patted his friend's back with a web. He knew how much Seezer had looked forward to rejoining his family.

Grub shifted his gaze upstream. "We have some real good eaters here, bro'. Real big ones, too." He pointed his bumpy snout toward Bartleby. "Hey, Lunch. Did you really swim all the way from up north?"

Bartleby held his head high. "Yes, I did, bro'. And my name isn't Lunch—it's Bartleby."

Grub chortled. "You've got spunk, red-ear. But Old Stump's rules are very strict. And one of his rules is, 'Bring him anything you catch.'" He glanced around before he whispered, "But my rule is, 'Swallow anything you can catch before Old Stump sees it.'"

Bartleby gulped. "Who is Old Stump?"

"He's the biggest alligator in this bayou—the strongest and the meanest, too." Grub darted another look upstream. "Who was the biggest in your bayou up north?"

"Seezer was," Bartleby replied quickly. He didn't add that there hadn't been any other alligators in their pond.

Grub flicked the water with the tip of his tail. "Wow, bro'! You must be strong, 'cause you're not that long."

Seezer smashed the water with his tail. The crack it made echoed over the water. "Ssstrong enough."

Bartleby waggled his little tail back and forth. "Seezer's not afraid of any creature," he bragged. He stretched out his neck and gazed at the quiet, sunny banks on either side of the stream. "Where are all the red-eared turtles? I thought there would be many of my kind here."

"Red-ears? Quite a few have, er, gone to lunch." Grub bumped up against Seezer once more, nearly throwing Bartleby into the water. "I'm about ready for a bite— aren't you?"

Seezer gave his jaws a snap that made Grub back away. "Ssstop your ssshenanigans," he growled.

"Okay, bro', I'll wait." Grub turned himself upstream. "See the great oak tree in the distance? The tall one at the edge of the water with a big knot in its middle? Old Stump's cave is just under the bank there. We'll have to ask him what to do with Lunch—that is, Bartleby."

Clinging tightly to Seezer's hide, Bartleby edged closer to the gator's ear. "*What to do with me*—what does that mean?" he whispered. He couldn't keep his voice from shaking.

"Sssurely, after ssso much ssswimming, I am as ssstrong as any gator here," Seezer hissed. "Just ssstay on my back and I'll protect you." He paddled closer to Grub. "Yes, I'd like to sssee this great gator for myself. Let's ssswim over there."

Side by side the alligators began gliding upstream.

"Wh-why is he called Old Stump?" Bartleby asked.

"Because he's thick as an old tree, and as stubborn to uproot as an old stump." Grub reached his tail across

Seezer's back. He gave Bartleby a little shove that almost knocked the red-ear into the water. "Not like you."

"Quit it!" Bartleby snapped. He was holding on to Seezer so tightly, his webs had cramps. But his insides ached even worse. He wished he'd never come here. How could this big bad bayou be home?

Old Stump

4

From a distance, Bartleby could see four tree trunks lying in a line along the bank. He wondered if Old Stump had lashed them down with his powerful tail or chewed them down with his spiky teeth. But as he got closer, he realized that the tree trunks were really alligators. The biggest ones he'd ever seen.

"Seezer, look over on that shore," he whispered. "Perhaps those gators are relatives of yours."

Seezer turned his head to see. "Sssweet Ssswampland! I hope they are relatives and not enemies." He took a long, deep breath. "Well, we will sssoon sssee. I sssuppose we have no choice."

When they were close enough, Grub called, "Excuse me, Great Gators. I've brought a guest to see Old Stump. Please—if you don't mind. And if he's not too busy."

The giant alligators all turned their heads toward Grub at once. "Of course he's busy," said the first one.

"Why should Old Stump want to see him—or you?" the second one asked.

The third one narrowed his eyes to a slit. "What's he doing in our water?"

And the fourth one hissed, "If he wants to see Old Stump, he'd better hand over that snack on his back."

Grub sank a little lower in the water. "But, Great Gators, my companion is no ordinary alligator. He's come all the way from a place called New York."

The first gator opened his jaws and yawned. His deep, dark throat reminded Bartleby of a cave—one he definitely did not want to explore. "Where's that?"

"Many rivers away," Seezer replied. "Ssso far away, it's where the geese fly to have their goslings each ssspring."

"Ha. No alligator can swim that far."

Seezer snapped his jaws together sharply. The crack they made caused the four great gators to twitch their tails. "Perhaps no alligator you know. But I am Ssseezer of the Mighty Mississippi. This ssstream is my home, too. It's where I was hatched."

"Seezer and I were probably even nest mates," Grub added. "Don't we look like bro's?"

All four big gators snorted loudly.

"I'll tell you what. Since we're kin, I'll let you give us that snack on your back," the first gator hissed. He slithered down the bank toward Seezer.

"I'm not a snack—I'm a present. But not for you!" Bartleby had had enough of these giant goons. "I don't think Old Stump would like it if he knew you were thinking of keeping me. You'd better go and tell him that we're here. Right now!"

The gators swung their heads together and grumbled to one another. The sounds they made were like distant thunder. "All right, all right. I'll go," Number Four said loudly. He skulked down the bank, dragging his tail, which had a single band of yellow at the tip.

"Hey, little bro'," Grub whispered to Bartleby. "That was very brave. Even if I could eat you, I might not. Too bad Old Stump's always hungry."

"Er, thank you." While they waited for the reply, Bartleby thought about his little pond in New York. Even in that cozy water place, the Claw, the Paw, and the Jaw had always been near. During the time he'd lived there, Bartleby had been captured by a raccoon, stalked by a snake, and mauled by a fox. But no enemy had been so big or powerful that it ruled all the others. Only when he'd lived in a tank had there been a boss—his boy, Davy.

Suddenly the bayou began to sway. Waves splashed over the alligators' backs. Deep in the woods, birds began crying their alarm.

"Is a storm coming?" Bartleby asked.

"That is no ssstorm," Seezer replied as a massive creature broke through the water. It was a murky, dark green

27

like the color of old mold. Its teeth looked as sharp and curved as fishhooks. The scutes on its back were as pointy as thorns. Its tail was almost as long as Seezer! When it opened its mouth, a rotten smell drifted into the air.

"Old Stump thanks you for the present. You may leave it in the water. Now go home." The giant gator's voice was low and slow. He definitely sounded irritated.

"But I am home," Seezer told the smelly giant. "I was born in this bayou, and I have ssswum many traveling waters to return here. Ssso has Bartleby."

"Well, you can *ssswim* right back where you came from. Old Stump doesn't care," the bull gator said mockingly. He waved his amazingly long tail. "Come on, Present. Old Stump will take you to his cave and add you to his stock of goodies."

"You can't sssend me anywhere," Ssseezer insisted. "My mother and all of my sssiblings lived here, although I don't know what happened to them. But I plan to ssstay—and ssso does Bartleby."

"Nonsense! There are already enough alligators in Old Stump's bayou—too many. Look! They are all starving. They haven't enough to eat." Old Stump cast a pitying glance at the gators on the bank.

"It's true, bro'. He doesn't leave a morsel around for any of us," Grub murmured. "Though I think his four guards sneak some of his food when he's not in his cave."

Bartleby's throat began to quiver. Probably the greedy old gator had eaten all the red-eared turtles that used to live here. That must be why he hadn't seen a single one.

"You don't have to worry about me," Seezer said. "I sssurvived in a place much less hospitable than this one. I ssshall be glad to hunt my own sssupper."

Old Stump emitted a long, stinking hiss. "Old Stump doesn't like you. You think you are special because you have traveled so far. You think you are strong and clever. But you are no match for me. Now hand Present over and get going!"

"Sssorry, Old Ssskunk. I will never give Bartleby to you."

"Old Skunk!" Grub chortled. "That's a good one, bro'. But you better look out."

Old Stump bashed his head against the surface of the water. It was the sign of a very angry gator. "If you don't give me my present, you will never leave this bayou alive!" he bellowed. "Old Stump will see that your bones are buried under the muddy bottom." The furious gator swam toward Seezer and Bartleby. His tail practically reached from bank to bank as he swished it back and forth. His jaws were open. Bloody bits of food were still clinging to his teeth. The air reeked of him.

"Wait! I'm not the eating kind of present," Bartleby cried. "I'm too special to eat. I'm a racing turtle."

With an earsplitting clap, the great gator closed his mouth. "What does Old Stump need with a racing turtle?"

"You can race me against other turtles. It will be fun. Don't you like to have fun?"

"Old Stump doesn't know. He's never had any. Besides, he's eaten all the turtles around here." Old Stump smacked his jaws.

Bartleby gulped. "How about racing me against alligators, then?"

"Against alligators? No turtle can outswim an alligator."

"If that's true, you have nothing to lose. But if I win, you'll have to let me go."

The moldy old giant stopped to consider. "All right. Old Stump can be nice. He can be patient." He turned his boulder-sized head toward the four alligators on the bank. "Whichever of you wins will get a minnow as a reward. *A small one of course.* We will hold the race here tonight when the horned owl hoots." He whirled around with surprising speed, whipping his tail at Seezer, Bartleby, and Grub. "You will wait on the bank across the way where my guards can keep an eye on you. Old Stump wouldn't want Present to decide to leave before tonight."

The Mysterious Friend

5

"I'm sssorry I ever brought you here," Seezer groaned as he paced back and forth on the mud bank. "This bayou isn't the sssame place I left. It's not home at all."

Bartleby eyed the four guard gators across the creek and shuddered in his shell. He was very afraid. But how could he blame Seezer? He'd wanted to come here just as much as his friend. "It's not your fault. Besides, I'm not giving up yet. A turtle is persistent."

"Little bro', you may be from New York, but you're not too smart," Grub groaned as he scratched the dirt for a worm or a beetle. "Not even the biggest turtle in the bayou is faster than a hungry gator."

"I may not be faster than those green goons, but I'm smarter," Bartleby retorted. "They're starving! If Old Stump keeps all the fish for himself, why don't they just find another home?" He eyed Grub curiously. "Why have you stayed here?"

The scrawny gator hung his head. "Guess I've been afraid that what's out there might be worse than what's right here."

"If we sssurvive tonight, we'll find a better place," Seezer vowed. "Come with us, Grub. Family ssshould ssstick together."

"All right," Grub agreed. "Although we may end up shmushed together—inside Old Smelly's belly."

"We haven't much time left to make a plan," Bartleby said. "I'd better take a nap."

"A nap, little bro'? Now?"

"Bartleby sssometimes sssees sssigns in his dreams," Seezer explained. "They helped ssshow us the way to this bayou."

"Here? Then we're definitely in trouble." Grub laid his head on the mud bank and closed his eyes.

"We'd all better sssleep. We'll need our ssstrength for later." Seezer sank down and tucked his tail close to his body.

Bartleby pulled into his shell and waited. Soon he felt a floaty feeling. Little flashes of silver appeared. He strained to see more clearly. The flashes began to form shapes—fish shapes! In Bartleby's dream, the shimmering fish zig-zagged teasingly back and forth. They blew bubbles at his snout. They glub-glubbed as if they were trying to tell him something.

He opened his eyes. Although the fish were gone, the

glimmer of an idea was swimming around his brain. But he needed help. He needed a friend who could fish and fly—a waterbird like his old duck friend, Mother Wak.

He looked along the bank and gazed at the sky. He didn't hear a single quack. Nothing flew overhead or stirred the leaves in the trees. "I'll never find a waterbird here. They're all afraid of Old Stump," he mumbled to himself.

"I might be able to help," called a soft voice from the woods.

Bartleby glanced at Seezer and Grub. They were still asleep. "Who are you?" he asked, craning his neck toward the tangled thicket.

"I'm called Quickfoot."

"Can you fish and fly?"

"No, but I am very fast."

"Thank you for your offer, but if you don't have wings, I don't think you can be much help." Bartleby edged his head back in.

"I have friends that can fish and fly. They might be willing to assist you."

Bartleby stuck his head out again. "Really?" He looked across the bayou. On the opposite bank, the guard gators were arguing over a crawfish. Suddenly one of them raised his head and stared across the water. Bartleby looked down at the dirt. "Can you come over here?" he whispered.

"Oh, no. If any of the alligators saw me, they'd be after me quicker than a fly can flit."

Out of the corner of his eye, Bartleby thought he saw the tip of a quivering nose behind a shrub. "What kind of creature are you?"

For a moment, the voice hesitated. Then it murmured, "A swamp rabbit."

"Oh. My friend Seezer used to tell me about the delicious swamp rabbits in the bayou." Bartleby took another peek at the sleeping gators. "You'd better go away now."

For a moment, a furry ear bobbed above the shrub. A shiny eye winked. Then it disappeared.

Bartleby's carapace felt as heavy as if it had turned to stone. He lowered himself onto his plastron. "Good-bye," he whispered.

"Don't worry, I'll still help you."

"You will?"

"Yes—I would do anything to thwart that greedy old gator! Once I used to swim and play in this bayou with all of my brothers and sisters. But Old Stump swallowed up every one of them when we were only youngsters. I've been alone ever since." Quickfoot's nose began twitching faster. "I will ask my egret friends, Billy and Plume, to come. Once, when their fledgling dropped from the nest, I hid him from the Claw, the Paw, and the Jaw. Billy and Plume were very grateful. I am sure they will agree to help now. But first, you must tell me your plan."

34

Snacktime 6

It was a moonless night. The sky over the bayou was as black as the pit of an alligator's stomach. For Bartleby, the darkness was a good thing. It would make it easier for Quickfoot's friends to land on the bank without being discovered by Old Stump and his guards. But the red-ear didn't feel very lucky as he floated behind the row of water lilies that was the starting line for the race. On either side of him, two hungry gators chomped their jaws impatiently. Unless everything went according to plan, he knew he'd soon be in Old Stump's gargantuan gut.

"When Old Stump says 'go,' you may start swimming," the monstrous gator bellowed. "He will be waiting for Present at the finish line—with his jaws open and ready." Old Stump's eyes glowed like flames above the blackness of the water.

"Excuse me, Old Stump, but did you remember the, ah, winner's prize?" asked Number One.

"A tasty minnow for the winner," added Number Two. He paddled himself slightly in front of the other alligators.

"But not too large," said Number Three. "I wouldn't want to overeat."

"Are there prizes for the runners-up?" queried Number Four.

"Old Stump would never forget to reward his loyal friends. The winner will get his minnow." The old gator flashed his teeth. "And the losers will each get Old Stump's sincerest thanks for trying. Now let's get started. Old Stump is beginning to feel a tad hungry. He will swim upstream to the finish line and wait." Swishing his great tail, he steered himself toward another row of water lilies near the entrance to his cave.

The guard gators began to thrash their tails, each one trying to get a head start. They snarled and snapped at one another.

"Get out of my way!" growled Number One.

"You slow, stupid thing. You might as well give up now," jeered Number Two.

"Oh, stop your fussing," Number Three told them. "You know I'm the fastest anyway."

"Perhaps, but I'm the hungriest—and the hungriest always wins," hissed Number Four.

Bartleby took a big gulp of sweet bayou air. Perhaps it would be his last. What if Quickfoot's waterbird friends,

Billy and Plume, couldn't find this hidden place on such a dark night? Even if they were late, it would mean the end for him. Maybe they'd decided not to come at all. Why should they risk a creek full of alligators in order to save a single red-eared turtle, anyway? It had been foolish to think that a creature he barely knew, and two he'd never met, would help him. He pulled his head into his shell.

"Bartleby, keep your ssspirits up," Seezer called from the mud bank. "I'll sssee you at the finish line."

"Good luck, little bro'. You're gonna need it," Grub added.

At the sound of his friends' voices, Bartleby poked his head out again. He smacked his webs against the water as hard as he could. "I'll try my best."

His four opponents snorted loudly.

"Present is going to do his best—I'd better start worrying." Number One snickered.

"Me, too. Present is going to breeze right by us with his great, strong webs," Number Two jeered.

Number Three splashed Bartleby with a front claw. "Better watch out for that little stub he calls a tail."

Number Four yawned. "Maybe we should give up right now."

"ATTENTION! OLD STUMP IS READY," the bull gator bellowed from the finish line. "ON YOUR MARKS, GET SET—"

"Wait!" Bartleby yelped. "The horned owl hasn't hooted yet. You said that's when the race would start."

"Don't be foolish. Old Stump is the one who gets to say 'go.' Now hurry, Present, while Old Stump's mouth is open. He doesn't want to overtire his jaws."

"Don't I get a last wish? You're supposed to grant my final request before you eat me."

"All right, Present. Old Stump can be fair. What is it?"

"I want to hear the horned owl's hoot one more time."

"So, you are a bird lover. Well, Old Stump loves birds, too—especially plump, tender ones." The gator smacked his jaws. "We will wait for the owl to hoot."

Bartleby felt as if he were no more than a fallen leaf as he floated between the other racers. In a little while, he would be free—or else he would be snack food. "I've got to believe in myself," he whispered. "I can do it." But the words didn't seem very convincing. He listened for sounds from the woods. Was something rustling in the treetops, or was it the wind? He concentrated on the water beneath his plastron. Did he feel the ripple of something entering the stream, or was that just his body shivering?

Hooo-hooo-hooo! Hooo-hooo-hooo!

"READY, SET, GO!" Old Stump boomed.

Using their long, muscular tails, the four guard gators shot forward. Bartleby took a big breath and paddled after them. He stayed low in the water, spread his webs wide, and stroked as hard as he could. But he couldn't catch up.

"YOU WERE RIGHT, PRESENT. THIS IS FUN!" Old Stump bellowed above the splashing.

Bartleby thought about giving up. "Why should I bother racing? I'll only get eaten sooner that way," he chided himself. "This isn't even a fair contest." But something inside him wouldn't let him quit. So he kept on swimming, even though the gators were getting farther and farther ahead of him.

Quag-quog. Quag-quog. From overhead, Bartleby heard a throaty croak. It sounded like a flying frog.

Quag-quog. Quag-quog. There was another one.

Without slowing his pace, Bartleby squinted up at the dark sky. Like black on black, two silhouettes dipped down and waved their wings at him. Now he could tell that they were birds. Birds with long, curving necks and wide, graceful wings.

"Plume and I have brought your delivery. As many as our gullets will carry," the first one called softly. "We'll release them into the middle of this bayou, just ahead of those four brainless beasts. Good luck!"

"Yes. Billy and I are so glad to be able to help a friend of Quickfoot's," the other added as she wheeled skyward again.

"Thank you," Bartleby whispered. He felt a new surge of energy. He paddled his webs faster and pushed against the water even harder. Soon the rhythm of his strokes matched the sound of his breathing. "Steady, quick! Steady, quick!" he grunted to himself.

In a little while, the excited whispers of the gators reached him.

"*Minnows! There are fish in the bayou. Enough for all four of us!*"

"*Quick! Get them!*" shouted another voice.

"*Where did they come from?*" asked a third.

"*Who cares?*" shouted a fourth. "*Let's eat!*"

Winners and Sore Losers

7

Bartleby paddled steadily toward the finish line. He swam right past the four big gators as they searched the water for every last fish. His limbs were beginning to ache, and the warm, gentle water made it tempting to slow down. But he knew he couldn't. At any moment, his opponents might run out of fish to eat and begin the race again.

He focused on reaching the end of the watercourse. In the distance, he could see Old Stump's eerie red eyes. How surprised the old beast was going to be if Bartleby won the contest. The thought made the red-ear swim even harder.

He was almost at the finish line when he heard snorting behind him.

"Ha! That turtle thinks he's going to win."

"That's funny! One of you should catch up to him. I don't care about winning that measly minnow anymore."

"Well, I don't feel like rushing, either. I just ate."

"Someone had better catch up to Present—or Old Stump is going to be mad!"

The four gators began swimming faster. Bartleby could feel their breath on his carapace, but he only sank lower in the water and paddled his webs harder. Never once did he turn to see how close the gator guards were. He kept all his attention focused on the chain of water lilies ahead that meant his freedom.

Seezer and Grub were waiting on the mud bank near the finish line. "It's hard to see, but I think little bro' is in the lead," Grub exclaimed.

"Bartleby!" Seezer called. "Ssspeed up a little more—you're almost there!"

When he heard his friend's voice, Bartleby made a last, great push. In another moment, he touched the row of lilies.

"Ssssweet Ssswampland, you are sssaved!" Seezer dove into the water and swam underneath Bartleby. As he came up, he lifted the red-eared hero onto his back. "Bartleby sssucceeded! He outssswam the others!" he bellowed.

"Bartleby did it! He beat Old Stump's goon platoon!" Grub whooped. He slid into the water to join his friends.

"You logheads!" Old Stump roared as the four gators straggled to the finish line. "You lost to Present."

"Sorry, Old Stump."

"I have no idea how it could have happened."

"I got a cramp in my tail."

"I ran out of breath."

"SILENCE! You are all good-for-nothings. Old Stump doesn't know why he puts up with you."

"It ssseems to me that they put up with you," Seezer said. "But now that Bartleby has sssecured his freedom, we no longer have to. Ssso long!" Carrying Bartleby on his back, Seezer began gliding downstream. Grub was right beside him.

"Stop! Come back with my present!" Old Stump bellowed. He whipped his tail at the four guard gators. "After them!"

The gators didn't move.

Old Stump smashed his huge head against the surface. "Then I will stop them myself," he hissed. He clawed and thrashed at the water as he began swimming after Seezer.

"Look out, bro'!" Grub cried as the massive body came hurtling at them.

As Seezer spun around, Bartleby was sent flying off his back. *Smack!* The red-ear landed so hard in the water, for a moment he was breathless. But Old Stump didn't notice Bartleby. His jaws were open as he lunged for Seezer.

Seezer roared and dove underwater. Old Stump followed. The bayou began to foam and churn so violently, Bartleby could only bob on the surface. Suddenly Old Stump and Seezer exploded above the water. They bashed their chests together as they slashed at each other with their claws, jaws, and tails. Their necks twisted into gruesome contortions as each tried to bite the other.

Old Stump flung his tail over Seezer and pulled him close to his odoriferous jaws. Then he dug his teeth into Seezer's neck.

Bartleby had been treading water beside Grub, watching the fight. Now he whirled into action. He dove underwater and paddled over to Old Stump's left hind foot. He bit the monster's outer toe—the most sensitive one on an alligator.

"Owwwww! That hurts!" Old Stump bellowed, pulling his jaws from Seezer's neck. He spun around. But before he could reach Bartleby, the red-ear dove underwater again. This time he clamped his small, strong jaws onto the outer toe of Old Stump's right hind foot.

"Owwwww! Owwwww!" the gator roared again. He kicked Bartleby so hard the red-ear flew out of the water and crashed down on the mud bank. Dizzy and dazed, Bartleby waited for his head to stop spinning.

Old Stump closed his jaws around Seezer's throat. He was squeezing the breath out of him. Suddenly another gator came swimming toward them. Its dark eyes flashed. Its teeth gnashed ferociously.

It's the end for us, Bartleby thought. Then he realized it was Grub.

"Let him go, Old Skunk!" Grub demanded.

Old Stump whipped his tail at Grub. "Stay out of this, you gutless gator—or you'll be next," he hissed through his teeth.

"Not unless you release my bro'!" Grub grabbed the end of the big beast's tail and sank his jaws into it.

Old Stump writhed, and wriggled, and whirled in the water, but he still didn't release Seezer.

Bartleby took a deep breath and dove in again. Once more he found Old Stump's sensitive hind toe and chomped down on it.

Old Stump's jaws flew open. "Owwwwwooooo, my tail! Owwwwwooooo, my toe! Owwwwooooo—OLD STUMP GIVES UP!"

Bartleby released his grip on the long, revolting toe. "My friends and I are leaving this bayou. Don't try to stop us, or next time I may swallow your toe," he said, although his stomach turned at the thought.

"Good riddance," Old Stump snarled. "You weren't a very good present, anyway."

The Flooded Forest

8

Before Old Stump could change his mind again, Bartleby, Seezer, and Grub crawled up the mud bank and slipped away into the woods. As he rode on Seezer's back, Bartleby inspected the tooth marks on his friend's neck.

"Do your wounds hurt much?" he asked.

"Sssertainly not. That old ssscoundrel's teeth were too rotten to ssstab my ssscaly hide very deeply. But I was getting awfully tired of ssstruggling with that ssselfish bully. It's good you and Grub joined the ssscuffle."

Grrruhhhh! Grub let out a proud bellow. "In the morning Old Stump is going to have a big tail ache. I wouldn't want to be around him then."

But there was no time to celebrate their victory. The thought of the enraged bull gator made them press on even faster through the thick tangle of vines and bushes.

Whoosh, whoosh!

"Did you hear that?" Bartleby asked from atop Seezer's back.

Seezer stopped and listened. "What did it sssound like?"

Bartleby's webs trembled. "Like the sweeping of a great tail across the forest floor."

"Like this, little bro'?" Grub whisked his tail back and forth.

"Yes—only with a much bigger tail."

"It could have been the sssound of mice rustling the leaves—or of a bird of prey sssspreading its wings," Seezer suggested. "But if sssomeone is ssstalking us, it's sssafer to keep moving."

Staying very close together, the little band scuttled around the trees, over logs and rocks, and through piles of brush. The deeper they went, the darker it got. After a while, they could hardly see one another.

Whoosh, whoosh.

"I hear it now, little bro'," Grub hissed.

"Ssso do I," Seezer agreed. "Sssomeone is trailing us. We must find a sssecure place to sssettle before it catches up." He swung his head toward Grub. "Which way ssshould we go?"

"I don't know, bro'. I've never been farther than the mud bank before."

"I know a swamp not far from here," whispered a familiar voice.

Bartleby stretched out his neck and looked around. "Quickfoot—is that you?"

"Yes," the voice answered.

"Who's Quickfoot, little bro'?"

"A new friend. She asked the egrets to bring fish to the bayou so the guard gators would eat while I swam ahead of them."

"Sssplendidly done!" Seezer looked around. "Ssshow yourself ssso we can thank you for sssaving Bartleby."

There was no answer—no crackling in the brush or soft, careful footsteps.

Seezer flicked his tail. "Come on, don't be ssshy. Time is ssshort."

"Quickfoot is a swamp rabbit," Bartleby explained. "Old Stump devoured her entire family. She is not fond of alligators. You must agree not to harm her."

"Why, I'm *very* fond of swamp rabbits," Grub crooned.

"Control yourself!" Seezer growled. He looked toward the thicket where the voice had come from. "You have my promise. If you ssshow us where to sssseek ssshelter, you will be sssafe with us."

Whoosh, whoosh. Everyone fell silent when they heard the powerful sweeping. It was getting closer.

"You can trust me, too, swamp bunny," Grub whispered. "Just let's get going. Please!"

"All right. Follow me." The silhouette of a plump rabbit emerged from behind a thorny bush. Before the gators could get a good look, it took off hopping.

The alligators had to scramble to keep up with the nimble creature. Atop Seezer's back, Bartleby was bounced and rocked. His poor head was starting to spin when he heard Seezer's webs make sucking sounds. "The ground is growing muddy," he told himself. "There must be water nearby." A bubble of hope rose above his plastron.

Just as the sun began to rise, they came upon the strangest water place Bartleby had ever seen. It looked like a forest. But instead of being rooted in solid ground, the trees were standing in dark, glossy water. Bartleby studied the quiet surface. More than anything, he was hoping to meet other red-eared turtles at this new water place. But he didn't see a single creature floating or basking.

"Doesn't anyone live here?" he asked.

Quickfoot flexed a soft, brown ear. "Oh, yes, the swamp is full of creatures. They're hiding because of Seezer and Grub. There haven't been any alligators in this swamp for a while. The last ones left during the dry spell."

"What's that?"

"A terrible time of great heat and no rain that makes the water disappear."

Standing at the edge of the flooded forest, Bartleby couldn't imagine how the water could disappear. It was everywhere he looked. Dry land seemed to be the thing that had vanished.

Suddenly a fish leaped up and splashed down.

"Sssweet Ssswampland, what a fat, frisky creature! I had better ssseize it before it disappears!" Seezer dove into the water.

"Save some for me, bro'," Grub exclaimed as he followed after him.

Bartleby was too anxious to be hungry. "I'd like to look for red-eared turtles. Do you have any idea where they might be?" he asked Quickfoot.

The swamp rabbit wiggled her fluffy tail. "Let's try the water-lettuce patch first. They often breakfast there." To Bartleby's surprise, she jumped right in.

"I've never seen a rabbit swim," he exclaimed as he slipped in after her.

She flashed a paw above the surface. "That's because we swampers are the only rabbits with webs between our toes"—she dove underwater and came up quickly—"and coats thick enough to keep us dry."

Bartleby took a good look at her dun-colored fur. Sure enough, water trailed off it in little streams, just like water off a duck's back.

In and out of the weird, swamped trees, Bartleby followed Quickfoot. Once, when he turned his head toward a splashing sound, he bumped into one of the woody bumps that surrounded a tall trunk.

"Ugh!" A soft grunt escaped from his throat.

"Better watch out for those cypress knees," Quickfoot warned. "They're all over the swamp."

Bartleby's insides clenched up tightly. *The trees here had knees. Rabbits could swim. And a watery forest could disappear.* Everything in bayou country seemed so strange. Maybe the red-ears would be different, too. He looked around for Seezer and Grub, but there was no sign of his friends. There was nothing to do but follow Quickfoot. He began paddling faster so he wouldn't fall behind.

The water lettuce was floating in the center of a large cluster of cypress trees with many woody knees. Bartleby's spirits lifted a bit at the sight of the big leafy plants. Each lettuce was shaped like a giant flower with lots of overlapping petals. He couldn't resist trying a bite. The thick, soft leaf was tender and succulent, and slightly hairy. It tickled the roof of his mouth.

"Oh, this is even better than the lettuce where I used to live," he exclaimed.

"Where is that?"

Bartleby paddled around. In among a patch of duckweed, three red-ears popped up their heads. The way they stared made him feel as if he'd suddenly grown wings or long, floppy ears. "I'm Bartleby. I came from a place in the north called New York. But bayou country is my true home."

"Well, I am Digger and this swamp is *my* home," one

of the turtles snapped. His ear patches were the dark red color of leaves in the fall.

"I'm Baskin and it's my home, too," a second turtle said. "Did you bring those two gators with you?" His voice was slow and deep, and his red ear patches seemed faded.

"Yes, those gators are my friends. The one with the shortened tail is Seezer. Without him, I could never have made the journey. We met Grub, the skinny one, at Old Stump's bayou on the other side of the woods. He was practically starving and—"

"Don't you have any swamp sense? Turtles and alligators can't be friends," Baskin interrupted. "You shouldn't have brought them here. Tell them to go away."

"I couldn't do that," Bartleby protested. "Besides—Seezer and Grub won't harm you. There are plenty of fish in the water for them to eat. And this swamp looks big enough for everyone."

Digger paddled closer. He stuck his snout in Bartleby's. "Baskin is right. We've lived here all our lives. *We know.* Alligators can't be trusted."

Bartleby edged his head in a bit. "But my friends and I don't know where else to go."

"Well, I'm not afraid of gators!" the third turtle declared. She was about the same size as Bartleby. Her carapace was a dark, glossy green, and its flared sides were decorated with a delicate pattern of green and yellow swirls.

Her ear patches were the orangey red color of fire. Bartleby couldn't help staring at them.

"I'm Lucky Gal," she said. "I got my name because an otter called Fishguts caught my right rear web—but I got away from him." She paddled around and poked her web in his face. It was missing two toes.

Bartleby stared at the wounded foot. His throat quivered. "I've never seen an otter," he admitted. "It must be a very dangerous creature."

"Oh, yes, especially to a turtle. Otters love to eat anything in a shell." In the time it took Bartleby to blink, Lucky Gal disappeared under the water. In another second, she reappeared on the other side of a lettuce plant. "To escape, you have to be quick and clever—and very, very lucky," she declared.

"Bartleby is quick and clever," Quickfoot said. She'd been so quiet Bartleby had nearly forgotten she was there. "He outswam four alligators in a race."

"Harrumph! You expect anyone to believe that?" a voice croaked. "No turtle could swim so fast."

Bartleby squinted into the floating lettuce patch. A large bullfrog was drifting among the plants. "You don't have to believe it, but it's true."

"*Quag-quog. Quag-quog.* Don't mind Big-Big," called a voice from overhead.

"*Quag-quog. Quag-quog.* Yes, that quarrelsome frog

would doubt anyone—even his own reflection," added another voice.

Bartleby looked up. Two great white birds with crooked necks and long beaks were perched on a branch overhead. He flapped his webs with excitement. "You're Plume and Billy, aren't you?"

"Glad to see you made it," the larger bird said. "Plume and I enjoyed helping you outwit those racing gators."

"Yes," Plume agreed. "We were tickled to have a chance to spoil Old Stump's plan."

Bartleby gazed at her huge wings and skinny legs. He'd never seen a more unusual bird. "Thank you. Without you, I would never have succeeded."

"What?" Big-Big leaped onto a plant in front of Bartleby. He stuck his puffed-up chest into the red-ear's snout. "You didn't say you had help."

"I didn't have a chance. I—"

"Harrumph! You said you swam here from up north. You said you beat four gators. I think you're just a big bragger."

Bartleby held his head up high. "Of all the swamp creatures I know, bullfrogs are the biggest braggers."

Big-Big's chest swelled up even further. "Why, thank you very much."

"But we red-ears are braver," Bartleby finished. He turned to the turtles. More than anything, he wanted to be friends with them. "If you would just meet Seezer and Grub, you'd see they mean no harm," he pleaded.

"I'm willing!" Lucky Gal paddled around to face the others. "And I have an idea. Let's have a swamp meet tonight."

"That's exactly what *I* was thinking." Big-Big hopped up and down on the lettuce plant. "Since we bullfrogs are the most hospitable creatures here, we'll be the hosts."

"I suppose a little competition might be fun," Digger said.

"As long as we don't have to work too hard," Baskin drawled.

"I'll ask Seezer and Grub to come," Bartleby said before the others changed their minds. "Er, what shall I tell them we're going to do at the swamp meet?"

"Why, croaking, leaping, and fly-eating, of course." Big-Big dove into the water and began kicking away with his powerful flippers. "We'll soon find out who are the real champs of this swamp!"

The Swamp Meet

10

Lazy as drifting logs, Seezer and Grub were floating beneath a giant willow when Bartleby found them.

"A ssswamp meet? That's sssilly!" Seezer snorted at the news. "We already know who the champs of the ssswamp are. No creatures are ssstronger than alligators."

"He's right, little bro'," Grub agreed. "Croaking, leaping, and fly-catching? Those things are for frogs. Who cares about them? A real swamp meet should have wrestling and tail splashing."

Bartleby squeezed between them and floated, too. "But if you don't come, they might think you're afraid to lose." He didn't mention that he wanted to show Digger and Baskin that they'd been wrong—alligators and turtles could be friends.

"Ssscared to lose? Alligators against frogs and turtles? That's sssenseless!"

"Maybe, but there's a bullfrog named Big-Big who thinks he can make a bigger splash than an alligator. And there's a red-ear named Lucky Gal who won a fight with an otter." Bartleby told himself it was all right to exaggerate a little, as long as it was for a good cause.

Seezer roared with glee. "Then they can sssplash and sssmash each other. That ssshould be very amusing."

"That's a good one, bro'," Grub said, whacking the water with his tail.

Silently, Bartleby drifted away. He didn't see anything funny. A wave of homesickness washed over him. He wished he were back in the pond up north with friends that didn't treat him like he was silly or dinky. Bayou country was full of rude, unfriendly creatures. It seemed as if Seezer was becoming one of them.

Later, when the moon rose, Bartleby paddled toward the ring of cypress trees alone. The water reverberated with the sound of the bullfrogs singing their boastful songs.

"We bullfrogs leap on super legs.
Our gals can lay ten thousand eggs.
From the air we snap up prey,
Or catch it if it swims our way.

"Be you dragonfly or lizard
you could end up in our gizzard.

Come and play!
Come and play!"

"I thought you'd decided to forfeit the meet," Big-Big called as Bartleby swam into the water-lettuce patch.

"We turtles don't give up." Bartleby hoped he sounded more confident than he felt.

"That's right—we're ready to play." Lucky Gal paddled out from behind a plant with Digger and Baskin behind her. In the moonlight, Bartleby thought her ear patches looked even more fiery.

Big-Big rotated his bulgy eyes. "What about your gator pals?"

Bartleby looked down at the surface. "I don't think they're coming."

"Harrumph! So their bellows are bigger than their bravery!"

"*Rrrum . . . rrrum . . . rrrum!*" The water began to sway as bullfrogs all over the swamp croaked with laughter.

Big-Big leaped up onto a big bouncy lettuce. "Well, don't worry. We'll start with something easy. The croaking contest."

"*Rrrum . . . rrrum . . . rrrum!* Never heard a turtle croak," the bullfrogs roared.

Splash! An alligator suddenly exploded into the center of the gathering. "Did I hear sssomeone sssuggest that alligators are poor sssports?"

Splash! Another alligator popped up. "I heard it, too, bro'."

"Seezer! Grub! You're here!" Bartleby exclaimed.

"Sssertainly, I am," Seezer replied.

"Wouldn't miss it, little bro'." Grub waved his tail at Bartleby.

Big-Big's eyes looked as if they might pop out of his head. "You're too late! We've already begun."

With the tip of his snout, Seezer splashed water at him. "You're not ssscared you'll lose, are you, bullfrog?"

Big-Big's wide mouth opened and closed, opened and closed. "Lose a croaking contest?" he said finally. "Harrumph! Of course not! I'll go first." He took a deep breath. A bubble began to form under his chin. It grew from the size of a berry, to an acorn, to a dandelion puff. Big-Big strained and the bubble grew larger. Now it was almost the size of his head, and then, a wasp's nest!

Just as it looked as if Big-Big might burst, he let out a croak: *"Rrrum . . . rrrum . . . rrrum . . . rrrum . . . RRRUMMM!"*

The earsplitting sound shook the water. It drummed against Bartleby's shell. He pulled in his head, squinched his eyes shut, and hid. When it was quiet again, he peered out at Big-Big. The frog looked as shriveled as an old leaf.

"Your turn," Big-Big wheezed.

Seezer sank lower in the water. Only his tail and head were raised. As he took a deep breath, his throat began to swell. Bartleby heard a low, threatening rumble. The water trembled. Then came a roar. It was as loud as the sound of one of the giant metal birds that sometimes flew overhead.

"Grruh . . . grruh . . . grruh . . . grruh . . . GRRUH! GRRUH! GRRUHHHHHHHH!"

The trees above the swamp shook. The birds flew out of their nests. Bullfrogs everywhere jumped out of the water and hid in the grass on the bank.

"Obviously, I am the sssuperior croaker," Seezer announced when he'd run out of air. "I win."

"Harrumph!" Big-Big rearranged himself on his throne of lettuce. "That wasn't a croak—it was a bellow. You were supposed to croak. You lose!"

Seezer flicked his tail against the surface. "Don't be sssilly. Alligators don't croak."

Big-Big jumped up and down. "See—you admit it. I win! I win!"

This time, Seezer's tail smacked the water. "You wart-ssskinned ssswindler!"

"You scaly cheater!"

Seezer opened his jaws and emitted a long, chilly hiss. Silence fell over the pond as the glaring gator and the pop-eyed bullfrog locked stares.

With trembling webs, Bartleby paddled between the two opponents. "Stop! Please! Perhaps we should call it a tie."

Crack! Seezer clapped his long jaws shut. "Oh, why not? Ssstrangely enough, I haven't had ssso much fun in a long time."

"Harrumph!" Big-Big settled back onto his lettuce seat. "I'm sure I'm having more fun than you!"

Fishguts Brings Trouble

11

When the contests, the arguments, and the feasting were done, Bartleby rested on the mud bank with the other red-ears. Together, they listened to the concerts the bullfrogs gave to boast of their skills at croaking and leaping, and enjoyed the twinkling lights of the fireflies. Digger and Baskin snacked on the juicy mosquitoes that swarmed the bank. But Bartleby had already consumed so many he ignored them. So did Lucky Gal. She was such a good eater that she'd won the fly-eating contest.

As the singing and chirping creatures began to quiet, Seezer and Grub disappeared in search of a last, whiskery catfish. Quickfoot retired to her hollow log at the edge of the swamp to curl up for the night. Digger and Baskin paddled off to bed down in the tall grass that grew in the shallows. But Bartleby remained on the bank beside Lucky Gal. He was too excited to sleep. He was brimming with questions about life in this place. Where were the best places to hunt for fish fry? Were there any snakes around? How far did the swamp go? But Lucky's limbs were tucked into her shell as if she were drowsing. Bartleby was afraid if he woke her, she might go away. Instead he soaked up the wonderfully humid air, and marveled at the yellow path the moonlight made on the surface.

"Come closer," the water seemed to murmur.

Bartleby blinked, but he couldn't see anything. He wondered if he was dreaming. It seemed as if the water were inviting him to swim along the golden trail.

"Closer."

The call was irresistible. He rose on his webs and treaded down to the edge.

Plop! He heard a noise. Rings of circles formed on the surface. They glittered and danced in the golden light. He waded in to get a closer look.

Suddenly he froze. A dark, sleek shape was flowing through the water. It was coming toward him as fast as if it were flying. He tried to bellow, or croak, or chirp. But the only sound of alarm he could make was a turtle's soft grunt.

"Lucky—quick, hide!" he warned as he pulled into his shell. He hoped she heard him.

A paw with five webbed toes and five sharp nails snatched Bartleby up. A flat black nose sniffed him. "Is that you, Tender Toes?" it asked.

"Wh-who is Tender Toes? And who are you?" From

inside his shell, Bartleby peered at the creature. It had a small round head with little half-circle ears. Its whiskers were longer than a catfish's. It smelled fishy, and musky, and dangerous.

"Silly! It's me, Fishguts, of course. I've come to finish what I started. Stick out your web!"

Bartleby curled his limbs up tighter. Above his plastron, his heart was leaping like a grasshopper. This creature had to be the otter that ate Lucky Gal's toes!

Fishguts licked Bartleby's carapace. "See? Green's not so bad," he mumbled.

"Stop! Put me down," Bartleby demanded.

"Sorry, Tender Toes! You got away from me once, but you won't escape again."

"I'm not Tender Toes. I'm Bartleby of the Mighty Mississippi—and you'd better let me go."

Fishguts held Bartleby up in front of his flat snout. "Oh, no—I couldn't do that. I have a yen for plump green turtles now. Especially one with three tender toes on her right rear web." He curled his tongue and licked his whiskers. "Don't I look hungry?"

Bartleby peeked at the sleek-furred beast. Its nose was twitching as if it smelled something bad. "Not really," he answered. "Besides, I haven't seen any three-toed turtles around here. Just tough ones like me."

"Too bad. Well, I will just have to settle for you." Fishguts raised Bartleby toward his open mouth. He touched Bartleby to his teeth. "Yum, I can't wait." He put his paw back down. "Er, let's go for a dip. I'll eat you while I float on my back." He grasped Bartleby tightly and slipped into the water.

"Harrumph! What do you want that rubbery red-ear for?" a voice called.

Fishguts twisted his neck around. "Who's there?"

"It's me, Lucky Gal. Your favorite three-toed treat."

To Bartleby, the voice didn't sound at all like Lucky Gal's. But it did seem familiar. He edged his head out a teeny bit so he could look around.

"Tender Toes?" Fishguts wiggled his long, tapered tail. "Where are you?"

"Over here, Wormheart."

"Wormheart! You'll call me Coldheart when I get you. I'll swallow you down like a minnow. And I won't share." Fishguts raised himself higher in the water. He still had Bartleby in a firm grip. "Can you see her?" he asked. "My eyes are not as good as my nose—or my teeth. Help me and I promise to let you go."

"All right," Bartleby agreed. He glanced around. "I think I see a webbed foot that's missing two toes kicking across the swamp toward those water lilies."

Using his long, powerful tail, Fishguts swam into the raft of fragrant blossoms. His sensitive whiskers swept the patch. "I still can't find her," he grumbled.

"Harrumph! I'm right over here, Mousemettle!"

"You won't call me that when you feel my teeth," Fishguts squealed.

Suddenly Bartleby saw a shell pop up. It didn't look like any turtle shell he'd ever seen. It was more like the shell of a large clam. Four broad flippers stuck out from under the shell.

"It's dinnertime, Tender Toes!" Fishguts cried when he spied the shell. He began to swim faster toward the odd turtle.

As they got closer, Bartleby saw the turtle's face. Its eyes were big and bulgy—not at all like Lucky Gal's tiny black ones.

"I've got you now!" Fishguts dropped Bartleby and dove after the pop-eyed turtle. His nimble webbed paw grabbed hold of the wide, flat shell. Big-Big swam out from under it.

"You're not Tender Toes!" the otter squealed.

"No, but I've got fast flippers," Big-Big bellowed as he kicked the otter in the nose.

Fishguts snatched at the bullfrog, but Big-Big disappeared among the lily plants.

As fast as he could, Bartleby swam down to the bottom of the swamp. Not a single ray of moonlight reached down there. It was so dark and murky he couldn't see a thing. But he knew he had to keep moving before Fishguts found him. With his long, sensitive whiskers, the otter didn't need light to hunt.

Bartleby stumbled along the bottom over smooth stones and sharp ones. He sank into a mound of mucky, moldering leaves that smelled awful. He struggled until he pulled himself out—and wandered into a forest of hairy roots.

"I've got to get away from here," he said as the waving roots enclosed him. But as he searched for a way out, he got twisted up in the sticky strands. They wrapped themselves over his carapace and under his plastron. They wound themselves around his left rear web. Bartleby tried swimming back and forth to free himself. But the more panicked he got, the more tangled he became. He tried to stroke upward, but the roots held him as fast as the jaws of a powerful creature.

The twisting and pulling was exhausting. Bartleby needed to rest and regain his strength. In spite of his fear, he closed his eyes. Maybe in the morning, Seezer would find him—unless the Claw, the Paw, or the Jaw found him first.

He awoke with a start! Something was nibbling at his rear web. He tried to jerk it into his shell, but his leg was still tied by one of the roots. Terrified, he tried to kick the nibbler away.

"Quit it!" a voice demanded. "Hold still! I've got to get you out of here."

Bartleby edged his head out at the peevish voice. "Lucky Gal, is that you?"

"Of course it's me. Now stop wriggling while I bite through the rest of the root, or I might miss and chew your web along with it."

"Okay." Bartleby could hardly speak. He was relieved and grateful—but he was also embarrassed. "My shell is tangled up, too," he murmured.

"I know."

While Lucky Gal gnawed with her strong, sharp jaws, Bartleby didn't move a toenail. In a little while, he was free. "Stay right behind me," Lucky ordered as she led the way out of the roots. "You've sure got a lot to learn about being a swamp turtle."

It was still dark when they broke through the surface of the water. Bartleby wanted to settle down with Seezer and Grub. The two gators were sleeping under the great willow at the edge of the mud bank. But Lucky Gal refused to get too close to the pair.

"Seezer and Grub wouldn't think of harming us," Bartleby told her. "It's the best place for a good, deep sleep. No otter would dare approach an alligator. We'll be perfectly safe there."

Lucky Gal cast a long glance at the motionless gators. "Maybe Seezer needed you as a companion for your journey—but he doesn't need you now. Here in bayou country, not even a sleeping gator can be trusted," she insisted.

Bartleby felt as if he were being pulled in half. He didn't want to argue with Lucky Gal. He'd traveled so far to meet other red-ears, and he wanted her to like him.

But Seezer was his best friend. Bartleby couldn't take sides against him. Unsure of what to do, he treaded the water with his weary limbs.

Lucky snapped the air with impatience. "I'm leaving. See you around." She began paddling away.

"Wait! Where are you going?"

"Bayou turtles don't announce where they're planning to sleep. You never know who's listening." Lucky Gal picked up speed as she sank down in the water. "I'll be in the lettuce patch tomorrow—if you can find it."

"You ssslept late," Seezer said when Bartleby poked his head out the next morning. "We're about to ssset out in sssearch of sssomething tasty. Come on."

"You go without me. I'm not ready." Bartleby took his time stretching out each web, and then his neck.

With the tip of his tail, Grub gave Bartleby's carapace a friendly tap. "The early gator catches the biggest fish, little bro'."

"Maybe, but I'm not a gator," Bartleby grumbled. "And I can find my own food."

Seezer swung his head around and gazed into Bartleby's eyes. "No one sssaid you couldn't. Perhaps you'd sssooner be with red-ears now."

Bartleby looked away. "No. I . . . I just want to be on my own this morning."

"Sssuit yourself." Seezer bumped against Grub's side. "Let's go! I sssmell bass ssswimming nearby. "

As he slid down the bank, Grub glanced back at Bartleby. "Better be careful, little bro'. This swamp's a big place. There'll be a lot of creatures out looking for their morning meal."

Bartleby gazed at the dark, meandering water. "I will," he answered.

But the alligators were already gone.

Bartleby paddled quietly in search of the water-lettuce patch. He didn't want to become anyone's "morning meal." His webs were alert for the vibrations of nearby swimmers. His eyes searched the surface for bubbles or ripples. But of all his senses, his ability to smell was the most useful. By sniffing and gulping, he could "tell things." When a breeze came by, he poked up his snout. Sure enough, he detected water lettuce nearby. Feeling pleased with himself, he began following the scent like a trail.

Before long he recognized the circle of cypress trees that stood in the water. He paddled up to them and ducked under a silvery curtain of moss that hung from a branch overhead. He wove in and out of the bumpy knees. Finally, he reached the patch of bouncy, big-leaved plants.

"Welcome," Quickfoot called softly. She had her paws around a large green leaf. "I'm glad you found us."

"Harrumph! Why be glad? Turtles eat too many flies."
Big-Big was perched on a lettuce. He flicked his tongue
out and captured a passing moth.

"*Quag-quog!* Don't be greedy! There's enough food
here for everyone," Plume said without taking her eyes
off the water. In another minute, she speared a silvery
minnow and tossed it down her throat. "The fish here are
fresh and sweet. You must try one."

"Right now I just want some lettuce," Bartleby said,
but he didn't take a bite. He was looking around for Lucky
Gal. He didn't see her fiery orange ear patches anywhere.

"Hurry up and finish your breakfast. We've got to get
going. I'm not waiting all day!"

Bartleby peered back over his carapace. Lucky was
right behind him. "I was blending in with the lettuce. You
swam by without seeing me!" she said.

He was so glad to see her, he didn't mind being teased.
"Where are we going?"

She spun herself around in a circle. "Everywhere. If
you're going to keep out of harm's way, you'd better get
to know every part of this swamp and every creature in
it. Ready?" Without waiting for an answer, she began
swimming away.

As the two red-ears paddled side by side, Lucky
pointed her snout toward things to be wary of. "See that
oak? A great owl lives there. You'd better not get caught

above the surface when she's out hunting. And that hollow pine is home to a raccoon. She's not much interested in big turtles like us unless she's got babies. Then she'll hunt whatever she can."

Bartleby liked being called a big turtle. He held his head up higher as he swam. Ahead he could see a log bobbing in the water with two turtles basking on top. One had deep red ear patches, and the other had dusty red ones.

"Hello, Digger and Baskin," he called out.

Digger turned his head toward the water. "Welcome! Isn't it a wonderfully humid day? The swarms of flies are almost as thick as the air."

"Why aren't you sunning yourselves?" Baskin grumbled without turning his head from the sun.

"Yes—there's plenty of room. Join us," Digger offered. "This is the best basking place in all of the swamp."

"We're going exploring," Lucky Gal told him. "Maybe later."

Baskin shot Bartleby a squinty look. "I heard they don't have logs like this up north."

Bartleby wondered where he'd heard that. "There were lots of logs to sun on at my old water place. But yours is very nice, of course."

"Huh!" Baskin grunted. "Well, I've heard the turtles up north are different."

"Um, yes, I've heard that, too," Digger agreed.

"Different?" Bartleby backpaddled a bit. "How do you mean?"

Digger gulped down a small, white fly as he thought. "Well, do you stretch out your right rear web or your left rear web first when you are basking?"

Bartleby considered for a moment. "Sometimes one. Sometimes the other."

"We always stretch our left first, and then our right."

"Why?" Bartleby asked.

"Because." Digger set his jaw and raised his snout.

"Ahem. Do you eat an earthworm head first or tail first?" Baskin asked.

"Whatever end I can catch," Bartleby replied.

"We always eat the head first." Baskin stuck his snout up toward the sun again.

"Phish!" Lucky Gal splashed the water with her tail. "I eat whatever end is in front of me."

Digger and Baskin both stared at her with their mouths open. But Lucky Gal didn't even seem to notice. "We're off to hunt fish fry now," she told them.

"Why bother? If you wait on this log, the mosquitoes will come right to you," Baskin said.

"Waiting is boring." Lucky Gal began splashing away. "And besides—I have to show Bartleby where the swamp ends. Good-bye!" Without another word, she began swimming away.

"Are we really going to hunt fish fry?" Bartleby asked

hopefully. He hadn't eaten any of the water lettuce before. Now he was starved!

"I always do what I say I will." Lucky looked back over her carapace at him. "Are you too tired to go farther?"

"Certainly not." Bartleby began to stroke faster. "I swam here from New York. Surely I can paddle this little swamp."

But the swamp wasn't little at all. Bartleby had to admire what an excellent swimmer Lucky Gal was. In spite of her damaged web, her strokes were steady and powerful. He wondered if he would ever feel as confident as she seemed.

"I hope you don't mind my asking," he ventured, "but how did Fishguts ever catch you?"

"The time after leaving the nest is the most dangerous of all here," she answered without slowing down. "I was just a hatchling when three young otters came turtle hunting at our swamp. The one named Sneak got my brother, and the one named Squeak got my sister. But I was lucky—I was caught by Fishguts."

"That doesn't sound so lucky to me."

"Oh, yes it was." Lucky Gal splashed the water with a front web. "The other otters gobbled up my brother and my sister, but Fishguts only held me in his paw. When his friends asked why, he said he hated eating green food."

"That does seem fortunate," Bartleby said.

"Yes, very! Fishguts might even have let me go, but Sneak and Squeak began to fight over me. 'I'll take that turtle—I'm still hungry,' Sneak demanded.

"'No, I should get her—the turtle I ate was smaller than yours,' Squeak retorted."

Lucky Gal was a good storyteller. Bartleby could imagine the two greedy creatures arguing. "What happened?"

"Fishguts refused to give me up. So his friends began calling him names like Wormheart and Mousemettle. They teased him until finally, he bit my toes. But when I cried out, Fishguts dropped me. As fast as I could, I swam down to the bottom of the swamp and hid until they were gone."

"That must have really hurt!" Bartleby's own rear webs twitched. "If Fishguts hates green food, why does he still hunt turtles—especially you?"

"After it happened, he became the butt of all otter jokes around here. He's determined to recapture me to prove that he's no coward." She paddled around to face Bartleby. "But he won't!"

"Definitely not," Bartleby agreed quickly.

Lucky Gal sank down in the water until only her eyes and the tip of her snout were showing. "We have to be very quiet," she whispered. "The fish fry are just ahead."

Bartleby held his breath as he followed Lucky Gal into the shallows.

Except for their dark, round eyes, the tiny fish were nearly see-through. But Bartleby and Lucky Gal sniffed them out among the clumps of water grass. The quick, slippery fry made a satisfying and delicious meal.

"It was a long swim, but well worth it," Bartleby said, when he was stuffed. "Thank you for showing me this place."

"Do you want to rest before we return?" Lucky asked.

After all the swimming and the eating, Bartleby did feel like a nap. He looked around. "Yes, but there don't seem to be any branches floating over here. And I don't see any basking rocks to settle on."

"That vine will do." Lucky pointed her snout toward a long, emerald green vine floating in a patch of duck-weed leaves. "Come on!" She stroked over and clambered up easily.

"All right." Bartleby paddled after her. He grabbed the vine with a web. It wasn't very wide, but the scratchy surface was easy to hold on to. He climbed up and balanced himself next to Lucky. The warmth of the sun began to soak into his carapace. His eyes began to close.

"I hope you're comfy," a voice murmured. It wasn't Lucky Gal's.

Bartleby jerked his head and limbs in. "Who said that?"

"I did." The vine bounced a bit. One end lifted up out of the water. A head with eyes as big as blueberries peered at him. A mouth that was purple inside said, "I'm called Curly."

"Lucky, quick! Swim away!" Bartleby cried. Faster than a frog off a mud bank, he plunged off the snake's back.

But Lucky Gal just wiggled her tail as if something were very funny. "We fooled him, Curly!" Her orangey ear patches seemed to grow brighter. "Bartleby, come back! Curly is my friend."

Bartleby didn't stop swimming until he was out of reach of the purple mouth. "There was a snake at the water place where I used to live. He pretended he was my friend, but he tried to eat me."

Curly swirled her body into two soft curves. "Don't be afraid. We rough green snakes only eat insects. Anyway, you're too big for my mouth. I was just having a little fun. I'm sorry I frightened you. Please come back—I don't get many visitors here."

Bartleby glared at her. "I don't think that scaring some-one is any way to make friends."

"You said you wanted to learn about this swamp," Lucky Gal reminded him.

"Not like that!" Bartleby snapped. He paddled to the edge of the water and climbed out. Without looking back, he crawled across the bank toward a thick, dark grove. He was tired of being teased about his lack of swamp sense.

"Wait! Where are you going?" Lucky Gal slid off Curly's back and splashed into the water.

"To explore on my own," Bartleby called. With his head up high, he plodded straight into the shadowy, forbidding forest.

The Whoosh in the Woods

13

Bartleby crept through the brush looking for the kind of place where earthworms liked to burrow—a shady spot with dirt that was cool and moist. He'd show Lucky Gal she wasn't the only one who could find food! He headed deeper into the woods, stopping here and there to scratch the soil with his webs. Along the way, he ate a brown spider and a juicy red berry. He used his carapace to roll a rock over—and discovered several fat worms nestled underneath.

Whoosh, whoosh.

Bartleby was sucking down an earthworm when he heard the familiar sound. Quickly, he crawled under a bush covered in kudzu vine.

Whoosh, whoosh.

The sound was coming closer. Bartleby felt the ground vibrate. He sniffed and gulped the air. He smelled danger. He knew what was coming.

"Bartleby, where are you? Bartleby, come on out!"

"Oh, no, no, no," Bartleby moaned to himself. "Please, please go away!"

Whoosh, whoosh.

In another moment, Lucky Gal wandered into the clearing, dragging her ruined rear web. She was a lot slower on land than she was in the water.

"Bartleby?"

A very large alligator emerged from behind a giant oak tree. "No. It's me—Number Four. Glad to meet you." He put one of his fat clawed feet over Lucky Gal. It covered up her entire shell.

"Leave her alone!" Bartleby scrambled out from under the thorny bush.

Number Four swung his head around. "Present! I've been looking for you."

Bartleby's throat was quivering as he crawled up to the gator's snout. "Let Lucky Gal go and you can take me back to Old Stump."

"I wasn't going to hurt her." Number Four lifted up his claw.

Lucky peeked her head out a bit. For once, she didn't say anything.

"Where are the others?" Bartleby asked.

Number Four blinked. "Others? Do you mean One, Two, and Three?"

"Yes. Are they searching for me, too? Or did they send you to catch me?"

"Neither! Soon after you left, I snuck away from them. You have no idea how tiring it can get being ordered around by Old Stump and those other bullies. You and Seezer were so brave and clever—it was positively inspiring! Why, even Grub showed some gumption. Right away I knew I wanted to join you. But I got lost in these woods."

"How do we know we can trust you?" Lucky Gal asked. Her head was up, but her voice was still shaky.

"Yes—at the bayou you were going to eat me," Bartleby reminded him.

"But I'm not really like that. I was only doing Old Stump's bidding. Won't you give me a chance to show you?" Number Four wagged his tail like an overgrown dog.

"You weren't going to give me a chance," Bartleby retorted.

"I can be better. Really! Please take me to Seezer and Grub."

"What makes you think they'd want you?" Bartleby scoffed.

"We don't need any more gators in our swamp," Lucky Gal added.

"Perhaps not." Number Four twitched his tail. The yellow band at its end flashed like a warning. "But if the dry spell comes, Old Stump and his guards will go on the hunt to find food. If they ever came here, I could help defend you. Three gators could keep you safer than two."

Bartleby had never known a dry spell, although he remembered Quickfoot mentioning it. He wondered if it was really going to happen. Then he thought about Old Stump's huge, smelly jaws, and his cave full of "goodies."

"Maybe we should see what Seezer and Grub think," he suggested.

Lucky snapped the air with her jaws—but she didn't protest.

Bartleby tapped Number Four's snout with a web. "My name is Bartleby. Don't ever call me 'Present' again."

"Well, this is a ssstinking sssurprise," Seezer hissed from under the willow where he and Grub were floating. He gnashed his teeth as Number Four paddled in behind Bartleby and Lucky Gal.

"What's he doing here?" Grub swam up to Number Four and snapped his jaws. "You didn't hurt my little bro' did you?"

"No! I wouldn't think of it. Bartleby is a hero." Number Four stroked Grub's back lightly with his tail. "I missed you, brother."

"Ugh! Get off!" Grub backpaddled away from him.

"He ran away from Old Stump," Bartleby explained. "He says he wants to join us."

Seezer struck the water with his tail. "You're a ssscoundrel and a sssneak. Why ssshould we ssshare a sssingle fish with you?"

Number Four hung his head. "Starvation can make any creature mean. But if you let me live here, I'll change."

"You're just saying that so we'll let you stay," Grub accused.

"No—I mean it. I could be helpful."

With his snout, Seezer poked Number Four in the side. "What can you do to ssserve us?"

"When a dry spell comes, Old Stump sometimes goes hunting. If he came here, an extra set of jaws could be useful. I'd help you fight him off."

"Who's Old Stump?" Lucky Gal asked.

"You don't want to know, little sis," Grub whispered.

"The creatures of this sssswamp have my word and Grub's that we won't harm them," Seezer said. "You must ssswear the sssame."

"I promise they can trust me, too. I'm really very gentle. I won't eat much. Just a few fish."

"*Phish!* I don't believe him," Lucky Gal declared. "I think you should send him home."

"I'll leave if you want. But it might be dangerous. If I go back to my bayou, Old Stump could force me to tell him where you are." Number Four cast a sidelong glance at Seezer. "I wouldn't be able to help it. I'm not as brave as you."

Seezer sighed a great, deep sigh. "I sssuppose it will be sssafer to keep him here than to sssend him back. We'll have to let him ssstay for now."

PART TWO

The Dry Spell

14

Bartleby tried to bask, but it was too hot. In no time at all, his carapace felt as if it were on fire. He slipped off the log he'd been resting on and plopped into the water. His plastron touched the sticky bottom before he floated up again. That had never happened before. Something was changing. There were no longer cool places in the water, not even in the shade, and the small fish that used to hide under the water lilies had disappeared. The mud bank was cracked and dusty, and the worms that had squirmed in it were gone. Even the air seemed to have fewer flies and mosquitoes.

With sluggish strokes, Bartleby paddled to where the water lettuce grew. The big bouncy heads had become shriveled little knobs. Their brown, wilted leaves made Bartleby's insides shrink, too. When he'd first come here, the patch had been busy with frogs, turtles, birds, and other creatures. Now it seemed deserted.

"Isn't anyone here?" he called.

"I am." Quickfoot paddled out from behind a bumpy cypress knee. Her ears flopped like wilted leaves.

"Why were you hiding?" Bartleby asked.

"Life is more dangerous during the dry spell. When the food supply grows scarce, hungry creatures come hunting for plump, tender rabbits." Quickfoot's pinkish brown nose twitched in the air.

"But Seezer will protect us. As long as he's here, we don't have to worry."

At the mention of the alligator, Quickfoot glanced around. "As the dry time goes on, Seezer and the others will grow hungrier. Then a friend may become a meal."

"Seezer would never eat me!"

"Perhaps not. But I can't say the same for me. A swamp rabbit is too much of a temptation for a famished gator. And this swamp has three big ones! I'm afraid I must leave for a while."

"But where will you go?" Bartleby began thrashing his webs.

"Deep in the woods where it is cooler and there may be ferns and bark to munch."

Bartleby thought about the dark woods where Number Four had once been lurking. "Will you come back?"

"I hope so. In the meantime, be careful, Bartleby." The swamp rabbit hopped out of the water and scampered across the bank. At the edge of the thicket, she stopped and looked back. "I didn't have a chance to say good-bye to Lucky Gal," she called. "Would you tell her for me?"

"I will," Bartleby answered.

But as he watched Quickfoot disappear into the woods, he wondered why Lucky Gal wasn't here. They always met at the lettuce patch in the morning. Had something happened to her?

He looked carefully under the lettuce plants and in between the leaves. He paddled in and out of the cypress knees. He sank down and combed the shallow, muddy water. He'd almost given up when Lucky came swimming into the grove.

"Where were you?" he nearly shouted.

Lucky Gal crawled onto a lettuce leaf. "I went to the far end of the swamp to look for fish fry, but there weren't any. Curly is gone, too." Her pert head sagged a bit, and her orangey ear patches appeared faded.

"Maybe you shouldn't go so far," Bartleby said. "Maybe you should stay nearby so the gators can come if we need their help."

"*Phish!* There's nothing at the far end of the swamp to worry about. And you can still find duckweed there to eat. Besides, I'm not calling any hungry gators to come help me. That would be like walking into their jaws."

Hungry gators. That's what Quickfoot had been worried about, too. It was almost as if everyone were blaming the alligators for their misery, when the real enemy was the dry spell. It was unfair, Bartleby knew. But Lucky's spirits seemed so low, he didn't argue. He climbed up on a plant beside her. For a while, the two red-ears rested side by side, drowsing and dreaming.

Lucky was the first to stretch her webs. "Let's dig for grubs at the edge of the woods."

"The last time we were in the woods, we had an unpleasant surprise," Bartleby reminded her.

"We'll just go to the very edge. I see a moldering branch that looks like a promising place to try."

"All right." Bartleby followed her to the thicket where Quickfoot had disappeared. There were still a few small, white grubs in the earth under the fallen branch. When they'd eaten all they could find, Lucky Gal headed back to the water.

"I'm going to visit with Baskin and Digger at their log. Do you want to come?"

"No. I want to spend some time with Seezer. I've been gone all morning." It was funny, Bartleby thought. Before he'd come here, he'd longed to be with other red-ears. And although he did enjoy Lucky Gal's company more than almost anyone's, he didn't always care to be around Baskin and Digger. He'd learned that creatures who weren't at all like him could be much better friends.

Bartleby began to paddle toward the giant willow. It was so broad and bushy, it stood out easily against all the other trees along the bank. Suddenly he stopped swimming and turned back around. "Lucky?" he called. "The next time you're planning to go to the end of the swamp, would you let me know first?"

"Why should I?" Her voice had the teasing note that could be funny—or exasperating. With her rear webs she kicked up a spray of water at him and swam away.

Gone!

15

Bartleby was drifting quietly under the willow, dreaming of cool, fast-flowing water. Suddenly he heard Seezer bellow.

"You ssstole my sssunfish!"

Grub swallowed. "Sorry, bro'—I was hungry. Anyway, it wasn't that good. Awfully bony."

"Why don't you go fish sssomewhere else? This is my ssspot."

"But I like it here. The sun's too hot."

"I'll move, I don't mind," Number Four volunteered. "I'll be back later when the sun goes down." Slowly undulating his thick-scaled tail, he began swimming away.

"Wait! Where are you going?" Bartleby cried out before he could stop himself.

"To the far end. It might be cooler."

Bartleby felt a ping of alarm inside. What if Lucky Gal were there? "No—it's not cooler at all. I've already been there." He tried to sound calm and reasonable. "You should take it easy in this heat."

Number Four flashed his sharp, crooked teeth. "Thank you for your concern, but I'll be fine." He kicked his rear feet once and took off.

Seezer flicked his tail at Grub. "There's ssstill not enough ssspace for me here. Find your own tree." He tried to sink lower in the water. "This ssswamp is becoming a mud puddle. My belly is practically ssscraping the bottom."

"Maybe your belly is getting too big, bro'."

Seezer smacked his jaw against the water. "You're the glutton, not me! Now ssscram before you're sssorry."

Grub opened his jaws, displayed his teeth, and hissed. But he paddled over to rest under a feathery cottonwood that was nearby.

Bartleby pulled his head in. He hated it when the alligators fought. He hated the dry spell. It was ruining everything here.

Later, as the sun began to sink in the sky, Bartleby swam back to the water-lettuce patch. It was the time he and Lucky Gal usually hunted mosquitoes. He snapped halfheartedly at a white-winged moth while he waited for her to appear. But though he caught it easily, its wings were so brittle, he could hardly swallow the insect down.

"*Quag-quog! Quag-quog!* Hello, Bartleby." A great white egret landed gracefully on a branch overhead.

"Billy! Where have you been?" Bartleby asked. "I haven't seen you in a long time."

"Plume and I are staying near the place where the river meets the sea. Food is more plentiful there, though a little too salty." The egret plucked at a long, unruly tail feather. "I told Plume I would come back here to check our nest. We'd like to return when the dry spell ends."

Bartleby's head perked up. "When will that be?"

"No one knows. It can be short enough to hatch a chick—or so long, every drop of water dries up."

All the water, gone! Bartleby's throat felt as if a lump of mud were stuck there. "But what happens to the creatures who live here?"

"Those that survive will find new water places. Already, many are out searching. I saw them scampering, slinking, and skulking as I flew over the woods." Billy flicked a few dried leaves from his nest, which was a rather messy collection of sticks and grasses. "Well, I'm going to rest now. I've promised Plume I'd return to the marsh early tomorrow. Good night."

"Good night," Bartleby replied, although it wasn't really dark yet. Birds like Billy went to sleep early. But Bartleby wasn't tired at all. Besides, he had to talk to Lucky. He wanted to know what she would do if all the water dried up. What if she didn't want to find a new place with him and Seezer? What if she wanted to go somewhere else? He settled down on a small lettuce plant to wait for her.

Night came with the moon and stars, but Lucky didn't appear. Bartleby told himself she had probably discovered something delicious to eat at the far end—a bed of gooey snails or chewy leeches. Or else, she'd stopped to talk with someone she hadn't seen for a while. In the morning, she would come back and brag about what she'd done. He wouldn't mind.

He paddled back to spend the rest of the night under the willow. When he saw Grub dozing beside Seezer, he let out a sigh of relief. He was glad to see they'd ended their spat. But Number Four was nowhere in sight. Maybe the ex–guard gator had decided to remain at the far end of the swamp for the night. What if the hungry gator was the reason Lucky Gal was missing?

"Number Four promised not to harm any of us," he reminded himself. "Lucky Gal will be fine. If she isn't back when the sun comes up, I'll go to the end of the swamp. I'll ask Seezer to come with me."

Quietly, he nestled against Seezer's tail and tucked into his shell. He soon fell into a turtle nap full of sharp, jagged teeth and tight, slimy places.

He hadn't been sleeping long when he sensed the water stirring. He felt a gentle push as Seezer's tail began to twitch. Bartleby poked his head out. Seezer was stretching his neck. He was tucking his legs back as if he were getting ready to swim. But it was still dark.

"Where are you going?" Bartleby whispered.

"Sssomewhere."

Bartleby tried to shake the sleep from his limbs. "Should I go with you?"

"No—ssstay here! Go back to sssleep. I ssshall return before morning."

"But where—?"

"Don't be a sssnoop!" Seezer hissed. He swung his tail hard and went gliding off.

What's going on? Bartleby wondered as he watched his friend swim away. Doesn't Seezer trust me anymore? The dry spell was making everyone act strangely. Some, like Seezer, had grown secretive. Others had turned solitary. And a few had become downright selfish. Bartleby felt as if his dream of finding a true home at last was shriveling into dust.

The Search

16

When the first morning light began glazing the sky, Bartleby swam past the sleeping alligators. Grub opened an eye and closed it again. But Seezer was sleeping so heavily, he didn't wake at all.

"Whatever Seezer did while he was gone last night has made him awfully tired," Bartleby mused as he paddled toward the circle of cypress trees. But he wouldn't let himself wonder about whether Seezer had gone hunting—or what he'd been hunting for.

As he waited for Lucky Gal at the lettuce patch again, Bartleby watched a water beetle spinning round and round in a small circle. Suddenly he remembered Billy's words about the scampering, skulking, slinking creatures he'd seen prowling the woods. "I shouldn't have wasted any time," he said, feeling as small and senseless as the beetle. "I should have searched for Lucky last night. She must be in danger. Otherwise, she wouldn't have stayed away so long." He remembered when she'd found him tangled up in the hairy-root forest. She hadn't waited for daylight—she'd come to his aid right away.

He dove off the lettuce and began swimming. "I'll find her," he promised himself. "I'll ask Seezer to help. Two pairs of eyes will be better than one."

But when Bartleby reached the willow, Seezer was still sound asleep. "Seezer?" Bartleby nudged him with his snout.

Seezer flicked his tail. "Ssshhh. Ssstop bothering me."

"But Lucky Gal is missing, and I was hoping—"

"I sssaid let me sssleep."

"But I'm worried that she might have gone to—"

"Sssilence! That ssscrappy turtle is no concern of mine. Now ssshut up or ssscram!" Seezer swiveled his head away from Bartleby.

Grub raised his snout and pinned a groggy gaze on Bartleby. "Little bro', don't waste your energy. She'll come back on her own. That gal is too tough for anyone to digest."

"Forget it! I'll go myself." Bartleby felt a hard, tight knot beating above his plastron. He didn't need the help of any lazy, big-headed alligators! With sharp, quick strokes he followed the route Lucky Gal had shown him. He passed the oak where the owl lived, and the hollow pine that sheltered the raccoon. He swam without stopping until he got to Digger and Baskin's log. Instead of drifting in the water, it seemed to be stuck in the mud. But the two red-ears weren't out on top. And there was no sign of Lucky Gal.

"Digger? Baskin?" Bartleby stuck his head under the dark, muddy water. "Can you hear me?"

"Why . . . are . . . you . . . here?" Baskin spoke more slowly than ever.

Bartleby swam around the log until he found a hole in its side. He sniffed and gulped. Then he took a peek. Baskin and Digger were huddled inside.

"I'm looking for Lucky Gal," he told them. "I'm afraid something terrible may have happened to her."

"She . . . must be . . . in-waiting—like . . . we . . . are." Baskin's voice sounded faint and far away.

"Yes. That's what . . . swamp turtles . . . do in the . . . dry spell," Digger agreed. "We hide ourselves away and have a good, long sleep."

"No—she wouldn't do that without telling me first," Bartleby insisted. "Won't you come out and help me search for her?"

"Not until . . . the rain . . . comes . . . again. We are . . . in-waiting," Digger said. "You should . . . go . . . in-waiting, too."

"I can't—not before I find Lucky Gal!"

"Go in-waiting," Baskin advised. "There is . . . nothing else . . . to . . . do."

"But there must be something," Bartleby protested. "A turtle is persistent."

"A bayou turtle . . . is patient . . . too," Baskin drawled. "You're an . . . outsider. You don't . . . understand our . . . ways." He pulled his head into his shell.

Bartleby's head was lower and his strokes were slower as he paddled away. Maybe he looked like the red-ears here, but he didn't think like them. He'd traveled all the way to the Mighty Mississippi to find others like himself. But he was still an outsider.

As he rounded the bend that led to the far end of the swamp, he wondered if Lucky Gal might really have decided to go in-waiting without telling him. Even though she'd been hatched here, he didn't believe it. She was too independent to act like the others. She was too lively to hide herself away in the mud for more than one night.

But what if there was another reason that Lucky had disappeared?

"Maybe if I'd been braver, Lucky wouldn't have left me," Bartleby mused. "Maybe she doesn't want to be found." The troubling thought stuck in his throat like a fishbone. But he kept on swimming anyway. He had to do everything he could to find her.

The water at the far end was so shallow, Bartleby's webs practically brushed the bottom as he paddled. He poked through the water grass, which had become dry and brown. He peered under a lonely lily pad. He looked among a cluster of smooth gray rocks that were rounded like carapaces. But there was no sign of Lucky Gal. The place seemed deserted.

"I'm too late. I've let her down," he moaned.

He dragged himself up on a soggy old tree trunk that was lying in the water. "Lucky Gal—where are you?" he grunted as loudly as he could.

He listened for a reply, but none came.

"Luckkkyyy!"

Beneath his webs, the tree trunk stirred. Something dropped onto Bartleby's carapace and pinned him down. He looked back. It was the tip of an alligator's tail—with a yellow band at the end.

"Number Four!" he gasped.

A big head lifted out of the water. Two rows of jagged teeth glinted in the sun. "Present! I mean, Bartleby. I—I didn't do it."

Bartleby's plastron felt as if it were being squeezed in a giant claw. He had to struggle to take a breath. "You didn't do what?" he whispered.

"I can't tell you. It's too terrible."

"What! What is?"

"You'd have to keep it a secret. If I thought you were going to tell, I'd be very upset. And when I'm upset, I become, er, snappish. Are you sure you want to know?"

Bartleby gulped. "Yes."

"All right." Number Four lifted his tail from Bartleby's

shell. "I'm so ashamed. I was going to share with the others. Really!"

"You ate her!" Bartleby dove off the gator's back.

"I didn't mean to. Really! But as soon as I got it between my jaws, it wriggled down my throat. Please don't tell Seezer and Grub!"

"Oh, Lucky Gal! Poor, poor Lucky," Bartleby moaned.

Number Four blinked his small, muddy eyes. "Did something happen to Lucky Gal?"

"Happen? You ate her!"

"Me? Eat Lucky Gal? Never!" The gator sank lower in the water. "I hate to think what Seezer would do if he thought I'd harmed her! No, I ate a tough old catfish that had been hiding in this mud puddle." Number Four heaved a big, wet sigh. "I know I should have shared it with the others."

Bartleby swam up to the gator and stuck his small snout in Number Four's big one. "I don't care about that!" he shouted. "I'm looking for Lucky Gal!"

Number Four paddled backward a bit. "Oh! Well, she didn't say where she was going."

"You saw her?"

"Er, yes—she passed by here yesterday. She was swimming faster than any turtle I'd ever seen. I called to her, but she didn't answer."

Bartleby paddled around in a circle. "Which way did she go?"

"I'm not sure. Into the woods I think."

The woods? Suddenly Bartleby wasn't so sure Number Four was telling the truth. "Lucky Gal wouldn't go there by herself! She's got too much swamp sense."

"I tried to tell her it was dangerous," Number Four whimpered. "But she was in quite a state. She kept muttering, 'I must get away! I must get away!'"

"Away from whom?" Bartleby demanded.

"I don't know. I was so frightened I hid in the mud. I didn't come out until you found me." Number Four hung his head. "I'm sorry."

Seezer's Secret

17

"That red-ear is too ssstubborn for her own good," Seezer said when Bartleby told him what happened. "Ssshe thinks ssshe is invincible. It's no sssurprise that ssshe's in trouble."

Bartleby didn't reply. He climbed onto a lily pad and pulled his head into his shell. There was a hollow feeling above his plastron as big and empty as a sky without stars.

"Sssweet Ssswampland!" Seezer's bellow was so loud it made the lily pads sway. "I can't ssstand to sssee you acting ssso mopey. All right! I'll keep an eye out for her later when I go hunting. If your friend is ssstill near this ssswamp, I'll sssend her home. Though ssshe'll probably sssay to mind my own business."

"Thank you," Bartleby said, but he still didn't come out of his shell.

"She'll turn up, little bro'. Lucky Gal is too smart to

get caught," Grub whispered. He nudged Bartleby's carapace gently. "You'll see."

On the bank under the willow, Bartleby heard Seezer stirring. He edged his head out of his shell. In the moonlight he could see Seezer stretching his neck and limbs.

"Seezer? Are you going somewhere? Can I come along?"

"Sssertainly not. There's sssomething I must do—alone."

"I won't get in your way. I'll just look for Lucky Gal. I'll be quiet."

"No! You must ssstay here."

"But why? We've always helped each other before."

"Ssstop nagging! My mission requires that I go sssolo. If I catch you ssspying on me, the consequences will be ssserious."

Bartleby didn't say another word. He just sank down under the water till he hit the muddy bottom. He felt as if a storm were trapped inside his shell. "Seezer isn't being fair!" he fumed. "He's using his size to be a bully! I don't think he likes Lucky Gal. I'm sure he won't bother to look for her."

Against his plastron, he felt the water lapping as Seezer's tail swept back and forth. He detected the vibrations of Seezer's feet as the gator climbed out of the water. In his head he counted minnows until he felt it was safe to surface.

Cautiously, Bartleby peeked above the water. He'd never deceived his friend before. But following Seezer into the woods was the safest way he could think of to search for Lucky Gal. Surely, no Claw, Paw, or Jaw would dare come out while a powerful alligator was about.

He glanced at Grub and Number Four. Both alligators seemed to be sleeping soundly. Holding his breath, he swam past them with small, quiet strokes. He hoped he would be in time to pick up Seezer's trail.

Bartleby's throat quivered as he entered the woods. He hated being away from water for long. He couldn't climb a tree, or run fast to escape from danger. But when he heard the whoosh of Seezer's tail sweeping through the undergrowth, he gathered his courage and hurried forward.

In the shadowy moonlight, the limbs of trees seemed to reach down as if they were trying to capture him. The long, eerie strands that trailed from them brushed his carapace like phantom fingers. Bartleby hurried away, climbing over the logs and rocks that studded the forest floor. Everywhere he went, he looked for Lucky. She was smart and strong, but could she really survive among the Claw, the Paw, and the Jaw? He was troubled by thoughts of Seezer, too. What was his friend doing here? What kind of secret was he keeping?

Bartleby was so lost in thought he didn't notice that the whooshing had stopped. He kept trudging onward until he came to the edge of a small clearing between two enormous trees. There was Seezer, snout pressed to the ground, making snuffling noises. Quickly, Bartleby hid under a thorny bush and watched. Using his powerful tail, the alligator swept the earth of leaves and sticks. Then he began turning in circles while he grunted to himself in a low, steady voice. With his powerful back claws, he tore up the dirt.

As he watched, Bartleby was overcome by a strange feeling. His webs began to tingle. His plastron buzzed like a hive of bees. He remembered a time in New York when he and Seezer had been searching for traveling water. They'd been exhausted from walking. They were so dry they couldn't go on. Then it had started to rain long and hard. As the earth beneath their feet turned to mud, Seezer dug a fine hole to collect the water—one wide and deep enough for them to swim in. The next morning, rested and refreshed, they'd been able to continue their journey.

Suddenly Bartleby understood—Seezer was planning to dig a gator hole! Only, instead of waiting for rain to fill it, he was searching for water under the ground. He was going to save them from the dry spell! Bartleby had to stifle a great grunt of joy. He was so excited, he scratched at the earth with his own small webbed feet.

But it wasn't long before Seezer stopped circling. Once more, he pressed his snout to the ground. His short, bowed legs began to shake. In another moment, he collapsed onto his belly. The moan he emitted chilled Bartleby from snout to tail.

"Ssso dry," Seezer whispered roughly. "Dry as a ssstone. Again!" Then he closed his eyes.

"Oh, no!" Bartleby gasped before he could stop himself.

Seezer opened his eyes. "If sssomeone's out there, you had better beware!" he hissed.

Bartleby held his breath. He hadn't forgotten his friend's warning. He didn't think he could bear to face Seezer's fury if his friend found out he'd been followed.

"As long as Seezer can still get angry, he'll be all right," Bartleby told himself. As quietly as he could, he backed out from under the bush and hurried away from the disappointed gator.

Ssserious Consequences

18

The next night when Seezer headed to the woods again, Bartleby was ready. Feeling a little braver, he followed his friend more closely. Seezer was nearly as quick on land as he was in the water, and Bartleby couldn't help stumbling, or bumping into rocks and roots, or snapping twigs under his webs as he tramped along. But Seezer was concentrating so hard on his mission that he didn't seem to notice the noise.

This time Seezer stopped in a place where many ferns grew. Bartleby hid behind a tangle of kudzu vine and peered through the leaves. Just as he'd done the night before, Seezer circled and sniffed, circled and sniffed. Then he dropped to the ground.

"Poor Seezer must need a rest. He's been working too hard," Bartleby murmured. He was determined not to leave his friend alone in the woods again. Quietly, he settled down to keep watch.

But as soon as his plastron touched the earth, Bartleby felt a strange sensation. It was so faint, he held his breath to make sure he wasn't imagining it. *Yes*—the cool pulsing beneath him was definitely real. It seemed to be calling to him from a deep, dark place.

Bartleby looked at Seezer again. His eyes were glowing. His head and tail were raised. His mighty chest began to swell. "Sssweet Ssswampland, there's water under this ground," the alligator bellowed. His cry was so loud it shook the ground under Bartleby's webs.

With his great jaws Seezer began tearing at the ferns that grew in the dark soil. When most of them were gone, he began digging furiously. His claws gouged at it. His jaws chomped. His tail mashed and scraped. Dirt showered everywhere like a sudden storm.

Behind the kudzu vine, Bartleby could hardly keep still. Though his nails were small, he could dig. With his hard shell, he could push rocks out of the way, too. He longed to help Seezer find the underground water that could fill a new home. But Seezer had warned him not to follow, and Bartleby wasn't sure his support would be welcomed. Still, as he watched from his hiding place, he couldn't keep from turning round and round, imagining he was excavating a big, deep hole.

By the time the night was almost over, both alligator and turtle were worn out. Seezer's circling and digging became slower. Bartleby's head drooped lower and lower.

Finally, Seezer sank down in the middle of the bowl he'd begun and shut his eyes. Bartleby crawled under the kudzu and slept, too.

Day after day, Seezer kept on digging. And day after day, Bartleby hid and watched. He wished Lucky Gal could see the home that Seezer was making. If she were here, he was sure she would demand to help. Already, the hole was beginning to look like a pond. All it needed was fresh, sweet water that was waiting deep underground. Surely, Seezer was going to reach it soon—he had to!

Yet Bartleby couldn't help thinking that even the most wonderful new water place would feel empty without Lucky. He still spent short periods searching the woods for her each day. But if he stayed away too long, Bartleby began to worry about Seezer. His friend hadn't eaten a thing since he'd begun excavating. He seemed to be in a trance—one that wouldn't let him stray from the hole until he finished it. He just kept on working until he couldn't scoop out a single clawful more of dirt. Then he would lie down and sleep—but only long enough to regain the strength to dig some more.

One awful night Seezer didn't awaken. Bartleby could hardly breathe as he watched his friend's motionless body for some sign of life. "A sleeping alligator is always as still as death," he reminded himself. "It's good that Seezer takes a break. Tomorrow he'll be refreshed."

Bartleby stayed calm while a big spider crawled onto the gator's back, thinking him nothing more than a fallen limb. He stifled a protest as a possum climbed down from a tree to sniff at the long, green body. But when a great horned owl swooped down and poked at his friend with its sharp, hooked beak, Bartleby couldn't stand it anymore.

"That fierce alligator is only sleeping," he warned. "You'd better flee before he wakes up."

"Hoo says?" the owl asked.

Bartleby crept out from behind the kudzu. "I do—a red-eared turtle."

The owl's round yellow eyes alighted on Bartleby. Was she sizing him up for a meal? He drew his head into his shell. But the cautious owl turned her head back to Seezer.

"He looks dead to me, but hoo knows?" She spread her great wings and flew up to a branch overhead.

Bartleby looked up. "You are smart to be careful," he agreed quickly. "Alligators are a tricky bunch. When they are hungry enough, they fool their prey into coming closer by playing dead. But I suppose you already knew that."

"Er, yes, of course I did. Owls are wise." The bird preened her feathers, which were as many shades of brown as the trees in the forest. "But thanks for reminding me. I've two young ones in the nest hoo still need a mother." She turned her head this way and that, inspecting the landscape with her moonlike eyes. "You should be careful as well. The woods are full of creatures that could make a meal of you. Hoo knows when the next one might appear?"

"You're right," Bartleby agreed. "I was just going to hide among those rocks when you flew by."

"In the rock pile? What a hooot! Though I suppose you'll blend in quite nicely." The owl opened her wings once more. "I must get home to my nestlings." Silent as a cloud, she sailed off into the night.

Bartleby crawled up to Seezer's head. "She's gone, Seezer. Don't worry about a thing. I'll stay right here and protect you while you get a good rest. You've been working so hard. Maybe I could bring you some food, so you wouldn't have to—"

Seezer's eyes snapped open. They flashed at Bartleby like angry sparks. "You red-eared sssneak! You've been ssspying on me!" he growled without raising his head.

"I only want to help you," Bartleby explained. "I'll do whatever you ask."

"Then go away. Ssshove off!"

"All right—I'll return to the swamp. But at least let me bring you back a fish. You need to eat to keep up your strength. Otherwise, you won't be able to finish digging—"

"Sssilence! Didn't you hear me? I sssaid beat it! This is my hole!"

"But I could push rocks out of the way. Or dig with my webs. I want to help make our new home."

"You sssself-centered creature. This isn't *our* new home—it's *my* new home. I've sssupported you long enough."

Bartleby's throat was pulsing so fast it hurt to speak. "I know you don't mean what you're saying. You're just tired."

With a great effort, Seezer stood up. "Exxxactly—I'm tired of taking care of you! You've sssapped me dry. Besides—you're always sssniveling over your sssassy friend! Well, go and sssave her—if you can!" He shoved Bartleby with the tip of his snout. "Ssscram!"

Bartleby was so stunned he didn't even tuck into his shell. His head was spinning with dreadful thoughts. *Seezer means what he said. I'm just a burden to him. He doesn't care about me anymore. He wants to be rid of me.*

In spite of the shock he felt, he drew up his head. "You don't have to push—I'm happy to go. I don't need you anymore, anyway. I can take care of myself now. And it will be easy to find companions who are nicer to be with. Since you came to the bayou, you've become mean and disagreeable. I don't even like you anymore."

Seezer didn't answer. On his wobbly legs he began digging as if Bartleby didn't exist.

Bartleby trudged off into the woods. But as soon as he was out of the gator's sight he plopped down on his plastron without bothering to hide. He didn't care what happened to him anymore. He'd lost his two best friends in the world. Seezer didn't want him, and Lucky Gal had deserted him. He wished he'd never come here. "I should have stayed in the pond in New York! At least the creatures I cared about were truly my friends," he moaned. Suddenly, more than anything else, he wanted to be back there.

"I could do it," he told himself. "The Mighty Mississippi would help me find my way back to New York. I've become a strong swimmer and a good hunter. I'm clever at escaping creatures that want to eat me. I don't need Seezer's help."

But for now he was tired. It would be better to start in the morning when he was rested. He crawled between two carapace-shaped rocks and settled down to sleep. "Tomorrow I will face my first challenge," he whispered as he drifted off. "I will have to find my way through the woods to the river without anyone to lead me."

Bartleby of New York

19

It took an entire day for Bartleby to find his way out of the deep, twining woods, and another to climb over the great mound of earth called the levee. Yet the journey back to the river was neither as difficult, nor as scary, as it had been when he'd first crawled out with Seezer. He followed his tiny but excellent snout toward the scent of the river—a delightful mixture of fresh and ancient waters, creatures finned and webbed, cushy-mushy mud, motor-oil fumes, and mysterious human junk. His long memory led him the rest of the way to the rock where he'd first climbed out.

Bartleby crept onto the stony shelf. He gazed over the vast, slow-traveling water. Its familiar brownish color was inviting. But before he dove in, he turned around for one last look at bayou country.

He thought of Grub, Quickfoot, Big-Big, Billy, Plume, and the others, and he wished he'd said good-bye. He felt sad knowing he would never find out what had happened to Lucky Gal.

Finally, Bartleby let himself think about Seezer and all that they'd been through together. By persuading him to come here, Seezer had given Bartleby the chance to be a real turtle—to live as a red-ear was meant to do. That life had been harsh, but it had been challenging, too. Sometimes it was even thrilling.

But now Bartleby wondered if he'd allowed Seezer to be himself. Alligators were such proud creatures. Was it possible Seezer had been afraid that he wouldn't be able to reach the underground water? Did he think he might fail? Had he been worried that Bartleby would be disappointed in him? Could that be why he'd driven Bartleby away?

"I should have been more understanding," Bartleby exclaimed. "I shouldn't have poked my snout in. I should have let Seezer be Seezer."

Suddenly Bartleby felt as if he were a hatchling just out of the egg—as if he were seeing things for the first time. Since they'd arrived in bayou country, Seezer had suffered terrible disappointments. He'd been chased away from his beloved bayou by Old Stump. And the brothers and sisters he'd longed to see had disappeared. Yet Bartleby had been too worried about himself to think about what Seezer had lost. He hadn't offered to help Seezer search for his family. They hadn't even spoken of it.

"Seezer was right," Bartleby whispered. "He guided and protected me, but what did I give him in return? I've been nothing but a burden."

He had to go back. No matter how difficult it was, he had to set things right. He needed to earn Seezer's friendship again.

"I'll just rest on this rock for a bit," he said as he settled down. "Then I'll get going."

"Cousin, are you there?"

Bartleby gasped at the familiar voice. Could it be the same, sly alligator gar that had tried to fool him when he'd first arrived here? He crept forward on the rock and peered down at the river. "Who is calling me?"

Through the murky water Bartleby saw a flash of yellowish hide. A long creature rose to the surface. It rolled its body over and over, churning the water until it was foamy. Then a gatorlike head broke through the surface.

"Welcome, dear Cousin," the cunning creature said. "You are just in time. I've caught a tender crappie, but it is much too large for me to eat. Won't you join me in the water and help me finish it?"

During his time in the bayou, Bartleby had learned a lot. He knew that most living things were creatures of habit—and that fish had short memories. This tricky gar doesn't remember me, he thought. He edged a bit closer to the end of the rock. "I don't believe you and I are related at all."

The gar raised itself higher out of the water and nodded—a nifty feat for a fish. "Of course we're related—I am an alligator and you are a turtle. We are both reptiles. Now please come and join me for a bite."

Bartleby backed away from the edge. "Not all relatives are trustworthy. Even if you were an alligator, you might eat me. But I don't think you are an alligator at all."

"Don't be ridiculous! Of course I'm an alligator. Look—I can breathe air!" The gar took several noisy, grunting breaths.

"I've seen fish suck in breaths of air while swimming near the surface," Bartleby said. "But those of us with lungs can do it on land."

The alligator gar snapped its jaws. "Are you saying that I can't really breathe? I can breathe as well as you!"

"If that is true, come out of the water and show me."

"I could—but I don't want to."

"Ha! Sounds like a fish story to me." Bartleby turned around and began crawling toward the mud bank.

"Wait! Just a minute! I will leap onto the ledge and show you. But when I roll back into the water, you must promise to come along. We must eat the crappie before some other creature makes off with it."

Bartleby thought for a moment. "All right—but you must promise that you won't try to eat me."

"You have my word," the gar agreed quickly. "Now just a moment. I'll need, ha ha, a running start."

As the creature dove beneath the water, Bartleby had a good look at its fins and fishy tail. Then he scrambled off the rock and waited far back on the mud bank. He had to fight a strong urge to hide in his shell again. In another moment, the alligator gar burst out of the water and flopped onto the rock shelf.

Before he could stop himself, Bartleby gasped. The gar was longer than he remembered—perhaps even longer than Seezer. It appeared to be nothing more than a giant head and a muscular tail.

"What's the matter?" the gar wheezed.

"I was right—you're a fish. You have fins where your feet should be," Bartleby replied.

"But I am also an alligator—an alligator garfish. Now let's go get that crappie. I left it on the river bottom."

Bartleby didn't move from the mud bank. "I'm not hungry anymore."

"You promised!" the gar hissed.

"You lied," the red-ear retorted. "You said you were a reptile and my cousin."

The fearsome fish gnashed its horrible teeth. "You think you can get away from me just because you have legs? Well, I'll show you!" It began rolling toward Bartleby. With a great effort, it flipped itself off the rock shelf and onto the mud bank. *Smack!* It landed on its belly and began rolling after Bartleby.

Bartleby was terrified. He scuttled into the thick grass at the edge of the levee and hid.

"Wait!" the fish cried in a pitiful voice. "Where are you going? Don't leave me here. Please! I don't think I can roll back into the river by myself. It's too great a distance."

Bartleby peeked at the gar through the tall grass. "Why should I help you? You were trying to catch me and eat me."

"No, I wasn't—really! I'm just lonely. Here I am, a fish with an alligator's head, an alligator's teeth—and the ability to breathe. Other fish are afraid of me. They hide when I swim near. Yet no reptile will accept me, either. I'm an outsider to everyone."

Bartleby knew what it was like to be an outsider. "Do you mean you've never had a friend?"

"Never," the gar whispered. "I've spent my entire life alone. It's because others always misunderstand me."

"If I help you back into the water, do you promise not to eat me?"

"I will treasure you always," the creature wheezed. "Er, what did you say your name was?"

"Bartleby."

"Please hurry, Bartleby. I'm beginning to dry out in the sun."

"All right." Cautiously, Bartleby emerged from the grass. "Can you move at all?"

"Not much. Without water I'm actually quite weak."

"I'll push at your middle. When I do, you must try to roll," Bartleby instructed.

"Do you really think you are strong enough to move me?"

"I am persistent," Bartleby told the gar. "Sometimes persistence is more valuable than strength."

"How wise of you, Bartleby. I thoroughly agree. With your help, I, too, will be persistent."

Bartleby crawled up to the fish's midsection. He wondered if the gar's skin would feel slippery or squishy. He pushed at it with his snout to see. "Your scales are almost as tough as a turtle shell!" he exclaimed.

"Perhaps you'd like to feel my teeth, too."

Before Bartleby could crawl away, the gar crooked its mobile head around. *Whap! Snap!* It grabbed Bartleby up in its jaws.

Good-bye, Bayou Life

20

"Let go!" Bartleby cried.

"Why, then I wouldn't be persistent! I went to a lot of trouble to catch you, red-ear. You were right—persistence can be very valuable." The gar clamped down harder on Bartleby's carapace. "But I always say, 'The stronger the jaws, the longer the life.'" Suddenly full of strength and energy, the wily fish began rolling for the river.

Bartleby struggled to free himself. He used the sharp nails on his webs to scratch the gar's jaws. He bit at its monstrous mouth. He wriggled and kicked as hard as he could.

"Uh! That hurts!" the gar grunted without dropping Bartleby. "Quit being so persistent and this will all be over much sooner."

The garfish's spinning was making Bartleby dizzy. But out of the corner of his eye, he caught sight of a human and a dog, running together across the mud bank. The gar saw them, too. It tried to roll faster. But it had been out of the water too long, and it was becoming weary. It was grunting harder and faster now. It was gritting its teeth on poor Bartleby's carapace.

As the human came nearer, Bartleby could see it more clearly. It was a man—a fishing man. He recognized it by its tall, rubbery foot coverings and the fishing branch it was carrying.

"Lookit that, Bertha!" the man exclaimed to the big, black dog that was running beside him. "That garfish is goin' as fast as if it had legs. I've seen 'em roll in the river, but I never saw one git out before. What a fish story to tell the customers!"

Mrrr-ruff! Bertha agreed. Which meant, "You bet!"

"Easy now, Bertha," the man said. "I don't want you tearin' up that gar. It'll make quite a tasty addition to the menu at Chef Jerry's. Lookit the size of that thing! It'll feed half our diners tonight."

Brr-ruff! Grr-ruff! Bertha barked. Which meant, "Can't we please eat it now?" She ran ahead of the man.

The gar's round, flat eyes appeared to get bigger. It picked up speed as it rolled.

Bartleby was afraid of dogs, but he was much more frightened of the gar. "That dog is right behind you," he told the fish. "If you drop me, I'll distract it so you can get away."

"Let it find its own dinner," the gar retorted. "You are mine. I've earned you." It rolled onto the rocky ledge.

Bartleby squeezed his eyes shut. One more twist and the fish would drop into the river, taking him with it. He heard the fish grunt with effort as it strained to flip over.

"YOUCH, MY TAIL!" it shrieked suddenly.

Bartleby's eyes popped open. He craned his neck around and caught sight of the dog. It had the gar's tail in its mouth.

"That's right, Bertha. You hold that fish. Don't let it git away!" the man shouted.

The gar thrashed violently on the rock, but the dog held on. *Grrr-ruffuffuff* it growled. Which meant, "I don't like you, Big Fish Thing."

"I don't like you either, Dumb Dog Thing!" The gar whipped itself around and snapped at the canine. When it opened its jaws, Bartleby dropped out.

YowoooOOO! Bertha howled in pain as the gar bit her short, floppy ear.

Crack! The man hit the gar on the head with the end of his fishing branch.

Yussssssss!!! The gar let out a sound so menacing, the man jumped back.

Splash! The gar flipped over and dropped into the river.

For a moment there was only the sound of water sloshing.

"Shoot, we lost that one, Bertha," the man said as he stared into the river. He patted the dog. "Well, it's okay, gal. That thing was too ugly to put on a dinner plate anyway."

Wuff-rrruff-duff! Bertha agreed. It meant, "Worse than an armadillo!"

Bartleby was still on the rocky ledge where the gar had dropped him. He was afraid to dive into the water. He was afraid to back up onto the mud bank. So he didn't move at all—he just hid in his shell.

"Well now, here's something we kin take back to the restaurant, Bertha," he heard the man say. Then a hand lifted Bartleby up and whisked him away.

PART **Three**

Chef Jerry's

21

In a truck as red as his ear patches, Bartleby rested on the seat between the man called Chef Jerry and the dog called Bertha. When the dog nudged Bartleby's carapace with her nose, Chef Jerry said, "Better leave it alone for a while, Bertha. I expect it's all worn out. This brave little critter put up quite a fight aginst that gar." With his free hand he reached over and picked Bartleby up. "See how the back of its shell is curved under? That means it's a boy. Think I'll call 'im Rocky."

Wuff-fuff-fuff-muff! Bertha barked. Which meant, "It's my turtle, too. If it wasn't for me, the fish monster would have eaten him." There was dried blood on her ear where the gar had bitten her.

"You were a big help, Bertha. You deserve an extra-good dinner tonight. I'll make sure you git the scraps left over from the nightly special."

With her wide pink tongue, Bertha licked Bartleby's

carapace. Then the dog put her head out of the window and let the breeze cool her ear.

Nightly special? Does he mean me? Bartleby wondered. He had to get away! But he was too exhausted to think clearly. The rocking and bumping of the truck was like the rolling river. In spite of his fear, he fell asleep.

He didn't wake up until the red truck stopped. "Welcome to Chef Jerry's Restaurant," the man said as he lifted Bartleby off the seat. "C'mon into my kitchen, Rocky." He tucked Bartleby under an arm and carried him around to the back door.

Bertha followed right behind them. Her mouth was open and she was drooling a trail of saliva.

Chef Jerry set Bartleby down on the counter. He filled a giant pot with water and put it on the stove. Then he filled a smaller pot with water and put it on the counter. "You need a bath before you meet our diners, Rocky." The man chuckled as he lifted Bartleby up and placed him in the vessel. With a scratchy brush he began scrubbing the mud and algae off Bartleby's carapace.

Bartleby pulled in his head and limbs as tightly as he could. A long time ago when he'd lived with a family, the mother had given him baths. But she'd never put him in a cooking pot.

When the cleaning was finally over with, Chef Jerry dried Bartleby on his apron. "Come on, Rocky. Let's go out to the garden. Maybe then I'll git you out of your shell."

Out of my shell! Doesn't he know that I'm attached to my shell? Bartleby began to struggle, but Chef Jerry only held him tighter.

"Calm down, Rocky. It's almost over." The man stuffed a round, leafy ball into one of his big apron pockets. To Bartleby it smelled like a new kind of lettuce. Was it a last meal to fatten him up? Bartleby didn't think he could swallow a thing.

The man also picked up a tool with a wooden handle and a sharp silver blade. He placed it in another apron pocket. Then he scooped up Bartleby. "Time to meet Princess," Chef Jerry said as they entered the garden.

What do I care who eats me? Bartleby thought glumly. At least the gar would have been quick about it.

From inside his shell he peered at the place. The garden was full of white tables and chairs, and Bartleby heard the sound of water trickling. He edged his head out a teeny bit. In the center of the yard was the biggest bowl he'd ever seen. It was made of stone, and it was filled with enough water to bathe Bertha. Inside the bowl, a fish stood on its tail. Water spouted out of its mouth and fell like rain.

Chef Jerry set Bartleby on the wide edge of the stone bowl. He put the lettuce ball there, too. From his apron pocket he extracted the shiny blade. He lifted his big arm and pointed the blade downward.

Mmmrph, mmmrph, mmmrph, Bertha whimpered.

"Good-bye bayou life," Bartleby whispered.

Thwack! Thwack! Thwack! The sharp blade flew through the air and pierced its mark. When the man was through, the lettuce ball was a pile of neatly chopped pieces.

"Here's some tasty cabbage to welcome you to your new home, Rocky." Chef Jerry leaned over the bowl and spread some of the leaves onto the surface of the water. "The rest is goin' into the nightly special—catfish stew." Gently, he set Bartleby into the bowl. "Now go on and see Princess."

Rocky and Princess

22

Bartleby sank down to the smooth, polished stones that covered the bottom of the bowl. He didn't poke his head out to look around. He could never live in a bowl again, no matter how big it was. He had to get back to Seezer! But even if he managed to climb out, Bartleby had no idea where he was, or which way to go.

Suddenly he was very tired. Maybe if he napped, he could dream the way back. At least if he was asleep, his loneliness would go away for a while. He pulled in his head and waited.

Soon the floaty feeling that came before a nap began. There were flashes of color and light. Then he saw a small oval pond filled with fresh, sparkling water. Tender green plants waved their leaves at him. Warm, squishy mud invited him to dig. Inside his shell he began to feel peaceful.

"Bartleby! Bartleby!" a voice called. Something shoved his carapace. *"Bartleby!"*

Bartleby struggled to stay asleep. He didn't want to leave the wonderful pond. But some annoying creature kept prodding his shell the way Bertha had with her snout. It wouldn't stop calling him. Finally, he opened his eyes and looked out.

A turtle was staring at him. She had a glossy green shell and fiery orange ear patches. When she opened her mouth, a stream of bubbles burst out. "Don't you remember me? I'm Lucky Gal."

Above his plastron, Bartleby felt a great ache. "You're only a dream," he said. "Lucky Gal was eaten. Or else she's back in the bayou with some new friends. You're not really her." He pulled back into his shell.

But the dream turtle turned around and stuck her right rear web in after him. "Oh, yes I am! Count my toes!" she ordered.

"Go away and leave me alone."

This time, the webbed foot kicked Bartleby in the snout. "Count!"

"All right. One, two, three, f—but there are no more!" Bartleby was so flabbergasted, it took him a moment before he could ask, "Lucky, is it really you?"

The turtle withdrew her web. "Of course it is!"

Slowly, Bartleby emerged from his shell. Under Lucky

Gal's shiny gaze he felt a little shy. "I looked everywhere for you. I thought I'd never see you again. What happened?"

"The same thing that happened to you, I suspect. Chef Jerry wanted a turtle for the restaurant's new fountain."

"Fountain? You mean this bowl?"

"Yes." Lucky snatched a shred of cabbage leaf that came floating by and chewed it quietly for a moment. "Do you remember the day I went to visit Digger and Baskin without you?"

"The day you disappeared," Bartleby said.

"Yes. I was on my way when Fishguts jumped out from behind a tree. He chased me all the way to the far end of the swamp and into the woods. I was so frightened, I kept traveling farther and farther. Then I came upon the levee. I'd never been that far before, and I was curious. I wanted to see the Mighty Mississippi. So I climbed over the levee. But by the time I reached the riverbank, I was exhausted. I couldn't crawl another step when Chef Jerry picked me up."

Bartleby nodded. "He caught me near the river, too. I was trying to escape from an alligator gar. Instead I got captured by a dog and a man."

Lucky Gal bumped up against his side. "Don't worry. You'll soon see this isn't such a bad place. Chef Jerry feeds me more than I can finish. There is never a dry spell in the fountain. And no shell-hunting creatures dare come near. Bertha sees to that. She's been my only friend here."

Only a dog for a friend? How different from bayou life—and how lonely it sounded to Bartleby. Although he was very relieved to see Lucky Gal, he could never be Bartleby of the Fountain! He would stay with Lucky for a while—but then he was going to escape.

As the two turtles nibbled the spicy cabbage leaves at the water's surface, Bartleby eyed the spouting fish at the center of the bowl. It was the shiny gold color of some fish in the swamp, but it had been out of the water longer than any real fish could ever be. And when he swam over and bumped against it, it clanged like Chef Jerry's fishing pail. Still, Bartleby wondered how even a false fish could keep spitting water like that without ever running out. It was amazing!

After Bartleby and Lucky Gal had finished up every bit of cabbage, they swam around the fountain. Lucky told Bartleby about the humans that would come to Chef Jerry's later to eat in the garden. "They're harmless," she assured him. "They only want to watch us. And their hatchlings can be very amusing."

Bartleby wasn't so sure he wanted to be in a place with hungry humans. And swimming in circles was beginning to make him queasy. He stopped in front of a crack in the wall of the fountain. It started out long and flat. Then it rose into a curve with two bumps that made it look like the head of an alligator. There was even a jagged part like a toothy jaw. Suddenly he felt like being alone.

"I'm tired. I'm going to take a nap," he told Lucky. He stroked down to the bottom and pulled into his shell. But instead of sleeping, he thought about Seezer. He wondered if his old friend was still angry with him—or if he ever thought of Bartleby at all.

At dinnertime, Lucky Gal called to him from the surface. "Bartleby, it's time to come out. The humans like to watch us while they eat."

But Bartleby only tried to dig himself under the stones at the bottom. He hadn't forgotten about the bath in Chef Jerry's cooking pot.

"Bartleby! The humans' hatchlings will feed us bits of Chef Jerry's delicious bread. They say he is the best baker in the city."

Bartleby didn't care about bread. But the thought of human hatchlings was pleasantly familiar. He couldn't resist taking a peek at them. Cautiously, he swam to the surface. He poked his head up next to Lucky's.

"I had three boys once," he told her. "The youngest one, Davy, was my best friend—though sometimes he could be rough."

"These young humans aren't allowed to touch us. Bertha doesn't let anyone get too close." Lucky Gal began swimming toward the platform that held the spouting fish. "Come on. The best view is from up there." She began clambering up on the sturdy shelf.

It was fun to watch the humans eat. "I think they have to use those silver sticks because their limbs are too short to reach their mouths," Lucky whispered.

"No—it's because adult humans don't like to touch things that are sticky or squishy," Bartleby explained. "But my boys always gobbled up food with their hands when the mother wasn't looking." For once he felt like he knew more than Lucky Gal. He eyed the diners as they ate piles of crawfish, bowls of lettuce, and big plates of gummy snails. "Sometimes the boys offered me little tastes," he said. But to his disappointment, the diners seemed to finish everything Chef Jerry brought them.

Their hatchlings were different, though. They finished their meals quickly. Then they came running to the fountain in the center of the garden. "Look—a new turtle! Princess has a friend," a girl with a yellow tail at the back of her head announced when she saw Bartleby on the pedestal under the spouting fish.

"He's awesome! Look how big he is," a taller boy observed. "He looks really strong."

Bartleby stretched his neck out as far as it would go. He held his head very high.

"Come on, let's swim for them. Maybe they'll toss us some bread crumbs." Lucky slipped off the platform into the water.

Bartleby plunged in behind her. After all this time away from humans, it felt strange to be stared at by them. But when he saw the happy faces surrounding the fountain, he began swimming faster. He dove under the water and popped up in different places to surprise the boys and girls. Once he even paddled backward, all the way around the big, stone bowl.

"Look—that turtle is moonwalking!" a boy cried. The brown fur on his head was as spiky as a hedgehog's. The other human hatchlings squealed with delight.

"Here, Princess," called a girl with curly black fur on her head. She tossed a large crumb of bread into the water. Lucky paddled over and snapped it up.

A small boy with the same tight black curls tugged at the girl's hand. "Throw one for the other turtle," he begged.

"All right." The girl tossed another crumb toward Bartleby.

Bartleby had tasted bread before, but usually it was bland and boring. To be polite, he nibbled at it anyway. "This is pretty good," he whispered to Lucky.

"Yes, it is. Every morning, Chef Jerry tosses out the day-old bread for the birds. They fly from all over to eat it."

The human hatchlings began throwing more crumbs. Lucky and Bartleby gobbled them up. But the smallest boys and girls couldn't throw very far. They just dropped their pieces over the side of the fountain.

Lucky Gal stayed near the center of the big, stone bowl. But Bartleby wanted more bread, so he paddled closer to the edge where the pieces were floating. As he did, he noticed a yellow-furred boy who looked like Davy.

"Look, I can almost reach him!" The little boy leaned over and splashed his hand in the water.

Bartleby backpaddled away from the wiggling fingers. Out of the corner of his eye, he saw Bertha rise from under a lilac bush and trot toward the fountain. With a gentle nudge of her big head, she lifted the hatchling's hand out of the water.

The boy laughed. He reached into the fountain again. Once more, Bertha lifted it out with a toss of her head.

RrrruFF MrruFF! she barked, but not too loudly. It meant, "Please don't touch the turtle. But you can pet me if you want to." She licked the boy's sticky cheek.

Yuck! Bartleby swam away before she licked him, too.

At the sound of Bertha's bark, Chef Jerry came out of the kitchen. He grinned at the hatchlings surrounding the fountain.

"What's the new turtle's name?" asked the girl with the yellow tail on her head.

"That's Rocky," Chef Jerry told her. "Looks like he's pretty happy in his new home, doesn't he?"

Crumbs and Champions

23

Bartleby felt a gentle warmth on his carapace. He poked his head out. Morning sunlight was streaming through the water. He looked around for Lucky Gal, but she wasn't on the bottom. Then he stretched his neck up and saw her yolk-yellow plastron floating at the surface. She was paddling slowly with her head down low as if she were stalking something.

Quietly, he swam up and scanned the surface. A fat moth was beating its clear wings against the water. Bartleby's webs tensed as he watched its fuzzy black-and-brown body bob up and down. He held his breath as the creature twitched its antennae, alert for danger.

Suddenly Lucky popped up behind the insect. Bartleby's heart pounced with her. "Yes!" he whispered as she grabbed the moth between her jaws. The sight of Lucky with wings protruding from either side of her mouth made him chuckle.

"Good catch!" he called as he paddled toward her.

Lucky Gal swallowed the rest of the moth. "I try to keep my hunting skills sharp—just in case."

Bartleby blinked at her. "I thought Chef Jerry feeds you more than you can eat."

"So what?" Lucky flicked her short, slender tail. "I'm still a bayou turtle. I still have bayou ways."

"Then let's go home!" Bartleby couldn't keep his webs from splashing the water. "We'll leave as soon as I see a route in my dreams. That's how Seezer and I began our journey from New York."

Lucky Gal bumped his carapace sharply. "Forget it. I'm not going anywhere."

"But why?"

Instead of answering, she turned and swam away. When she did, Bartleby could see her ruined rear web.

"What a beetlebrain I am," he moaned. "Lucky is so capable in the water, I forgot about her missing toes. She could never crawl all the way home from here."

In the afternoon, Bartleby saw the red truck roll into the driveway that ran along the side of the restaurant. Bertha jumped out and came running up to the fountain. *Prrruh! Prrruh!* came a rumble from deep in her throat. It meant, "Princess!"

Lucky swam to the edge. "Hi, Bertha. What's the news?"

Mrrruff, rrruff! Bertha barked. It meant, "Yummy rabbit stew for dinner tonight."

"Rabbit! Yuck!" Bartleby whispered under his breath.

Bertha's dark eyes widened until the whites showed. Her hearing was better than Bartleby realized. *RrrrrRrrrr-Rrrr,* she crooned. It meant, "Don't worry. Plenty of fish and veggies, too."

"Thanks," Bartleby replied. He hadn't meant to hurt her feelings.

"Let's all bask," Lucky Gal said. She hauled herself up onto the wide stone rim of the fountain, right next to Bertha. The dog leaned over and licked Lucky's carapace.

"C'mon up, Rrrocky!" Lucky called. The teasing tone was back in her voice.

A tiny sigh escaped from Bartleby's throat. He still didn't like dogs much. But he was relieved that Lucky wasn't upset with him anymore. He dug his claws into the stone and climbed onto the ledge. Once more, Bertha leaned over. When he saw her pink tongue coming, Bartleby squinched his eyes shut—but this time he stifled his *yuck!*

Side by side, Bartleby and Lucky Gal settled onto their plastrons and basked on the edge. Bertha lay down in the grass beside the fountain and soaked up the sun, too. The dog didn't say much as Bartleby and Lucky discussed their memories of swamp life. But Bartleby could tell by the way she kept her ears cocked that Bertha was listening.

Later, when the dinner guests arrived, Bartleby didn't hide. He followed Lucky Gal to the center of the fountain and crawled onto the pedestal that held the spouting fish. There seemed to be even more human hatchlings at the tables than there'd been the night before.

Eagerly, Bartleby watched the diners. The mothers and fathers ate hungrily from their plates, but the boys and girls only seemed to pick at the food. Some of them stuffed bread in their pockets when they thought no one was looking. Others bounced up and down in their chairs as if they couldn't hold still. Bartleby felt like bouncing, too. Inside his shell, his body twitched as he waited on the platform for them to finish eating.

A skinny boy was the first to jump off his chair and run to the fountain. "Princess! Rocky!" he called. He held up a piece of bread and pulled off a crumb. The other human hatchlings in the garden turned in their chairs and stared.

On the platform, Bartleby and Lucky Gal rose on their webs and stretched their heads forward. The boy pulled back his arm and threw the crumb in a wide arc. Before it even landed, Lucky dove in.

She'd already begun swimming when Bartleby started after her. He lowered his head in the water and paddled hard. He didn't care about the bread, but he did want to win. He didn't take a breath till he was nearly side by side with her. But when she saw him, Lucky began stroking even more furiously toward the bobbing crumb.

"C'mon, Princess, hurry!" Bartleby heard the boy call.

"C'mon, Rocky, you can beat her!" another one shouted.

"Awesome! It's a turtle race!" a third voice piped.

Bartleby glanced up for a moment. It looked like all the human hatchlings had gathered at the fountain. Some of the mothers and fathers were right behind them. Bertha was wedged in between a boy and a girl, barking, *Wufff, wufff, wufff.* It meant, "Go, go, go!"

But Bartleby didn't really mind the noisy crowd of humans. In fact, he liked them. And they all seemed to like him, too. They admired how strong he was, how handsome, and how fast he could swim. He felt . . . *important.*

Lucky Gal didn't pay attention to the cheers. She kept on swimming without letting her attention slip from the prize for a single moment. To catch up, Bartleby had to pull harder with his webs.

Neck and neck, the two turtles streaked through the water. When the crumb was just a few strokes away, Bartleby took a breath and dove beneath the surface. He wanted to snatch the bread from underneath the water. But when he got there, Lucky had already snapped up the morsel. She held it between her jaws for a moment before she gulped it down.

The humans began clapping their hands.

"Princess rocks!" a boy shouted.

"Turtles rock!" another hatchling added.

Bertha was still barking, *Wufff, wufff, wufff!*

Chef Jerry came into the garden and joined the crowd. "What's all this ruckus?" he asked.

"Princess and Rocky just raced for a bread crumb—and Princess won," a girl replied.

Chef Jerry got a broad grin on his face. "Well, then Rocky needs a rematch."

Bartleby perked up his head. He did need another chance. He'd been foolish to let himself be distracted by the humans. In the bayou, a slip like that could have cost him his life.

"I'll throw another crumb," a boy shouted as he ran around to the opposite side.

"Bartleby, come on—get ready!" Lucky Gal's webs were patting the water and her tail was wriggling.

"All right." Bartleby swam up beside her. Seeing Lucky so excited and happy, he found he didn't mind losing the first match to her. But the next time, he was planning to win!

The Red Streak

24

Each night it seemed to Bartleby that Chef Jerry's restaurant got busier. The human hatchlings jostled for places to stand around the fountain and argued over who would throw the first crumb. Chef Jerry had to keep the restaurant open later to serve all the diners. And Bartleby and Lucky Gal began having not just two crumb races, but six, or eight, or ten—until finally, all the humans went home.

Bartleby was no longer frightened when Chef Jerry came to the fountain with a pot in his hands. The man called Bartleby and Lucky his "star athletes"—whatever those were. And the pot held the choicest pieces of fish and the freshest greens from the man's kitchen. There was always more than the turtles could eat, so they saved their leftovers for Bertha. Even though Chef Jerry fed her big bowls of food, she always had room for one more mouthful.

Afterward, Bartleby and Lucky Gal would bask on the

ledge of the fountain while Bertha stretched out on the grass below. They talked less and less of the swamp, and more about which of the boys and girls who came regularly were their favorites, or whether crawdad or trout was tastier.

But when Bartleby napped, he still dreamed of bayou country. He would see flashes of a small, clear pond surrounded by finger-leaved ferns and purple-flowering vines. He glimpsed a funny palmetto tree with leaves that looked like a turkey's tail, and a slender young willow that reminded him of the one at his old swamp. Sometimes he saw Seezer and Grub lying together on a sunny mud bank—with just enough room for him to fit in between them. But the dream always ended suddenly with a streak of red that blurred everything else. Then Bartleby would awaken with his heart pounding against his plastron.

One morning, he was dozing on the warm, wide fountain rim when he thought he heard something.

Quag-quog! Quag-quog!

Bartleby opened his eyes and looked up. All he saw was a fast-moving cloud.

Quag-quog! Quag-quog!

Could it be? Bartleby stood on his webs and stretched up his neck. As the cloud came closer, he could see it was actually a great white bird. His throat began to quiver. "Billy?"

"*Quag-quog! Quag-quog!* Bartleby! I've been searching everywhere for you."

The bird began gliding down toward the fountain. Suddenly Bertha jumped up and pushed Bartleby into the water.

Gruff, ruff, ruff, mrrrrrrUFF! she barked in her deepest voice. It meant, "Stay away from my turtle, big bird, or I'll turn you into a pile of feathers!"

The bird flapped its wings, and rose out of reach.

"Bertha, wait! That bird is my friend," Bartleby grunted loudly.

But Bertha continued to growl. The whites of her eyes were showing. *Grrrrrrrr, errrrrrr.* It meant, "That skinny-legged bird has an awfully sharp beak."

Lucky swam up beside Bartleby. "Don't worry, Bertha. It won't harm us." She poked her snout in the air. "Billy! Welcome!" she grunted.

Under Bertha's watchful gaze, the egret landed on the high, white fence that surrounded the garden. He twisted his long, graceful neck and cocked his head.

"*Quag-quog! Quag-quog!* You don't know how glad I am to see you! Though I never expected to find you both together."

"Oh Billy, it's good to see you, too," Bartleby exclaimed. "I want to hear everything that is happening in the bayou."

Lucky Gal chuckled softly. "I suspect that will take all morning. I'll leave you two friends to talk while I bask."

She slipped back into the water and swam toward the pedestal.

"First tell me why you were looking for me. Is something the matter?" Bartleby asked.

"Many creatures at Friendship Hole have volunteered to hunt for you. But only we birds can search as far as the city." As if to demonstrate, Billy spread his brilliant white wings.

"Friendship Hole?" Bartleby asked. He felt a bit confused. "What is that?"

"It's what we've named the gator hole that Seezer dug for us when our swamp dried up. The hole is now a wonderful pond. Many of your old friends live there."

"He made it big enough for everyone?" Bartleby whispered.

Billy bowed his head. "It's the best gator hole I've ever seen—and the deepest. Full of sweet, clear water from under the ground."

"He did it! Seezer finished the gator hole!" Bartleby was so excited he fell back into the water.

Quag-quog! Billy called in a mournful voice. "In spite of our beautiful home, there is bad news."

Bartleby thought of the red streak that always ended his dreams. Suddenly he could hardly speak. "Has something happened to Seezer?"

"Happened? Not exactly. But since you left the bayou, he's suffered greatly." Billy tucked his head down against his chest. "He says he can't forget the terrible things he said to you. He's certain you will never forgive him."

"But I do forgive him! I said some awful things as well," Bartleby cried. He splashed the water with all four webs. "Hurry, Billy. Fly back and tell Seezer that I am sorry, too."

"*Quag-quog*. I'm afraid it's too late for messages now. Seezer stays in his cave at the end of the pond and won't come out. He refuses to eat a bite, or let anyone but Grub draw near. But perhaps if you came, you could persuade him."

Bartleby glanced back over his carapace at Lucky Gal. She seemed to be asleep on the platform under the fish. "I can't leave right now. Perhaps sometime in the future . . ."

"There's no time—Seezer is growing weaker each day."

"But he has Grub and Number Four to care for him. He doesn't really need me anymore."

Billy drew himself up and puffed out his chest. "You have my sympathy, Bartleby. It's sad to see you imprisoned in this garden." He shot a sharp gaze at Bertha. She was lying quietly in the grass beneath the fountain, but her eyes were open and her ears were twitching.

"I'm not a prisoner!" Bartleby protested. "I could get out if I wanted to."

Billy pecked under a wing. "I see. Living in the city must be very nice—especially near a human feeding station like this one. I've heard the pigeons say the bread crumbs are very tasty. But I could never stay. *Quag-quog!* I'd miss the smell of kudzu flowers, and the sound the breeze makes in the trees. I'd be lonely for my family and friends."

"Lucky Gal and Bertha are my friends, too," Bartleby said. But he couldn't help edging his head in.

"*Quag-quog!* It's just as well that you are satisfied with your life. Without wings, you'd never be able to find your way to Friendship Hole. It is too far and too well hidden."

"I found my way here from New York, a place that is many rivers away. Surely I would be able to find Seezer's hole," Bartleby replied. But an ache was spreading above his plastron.

"Yes, but on that trip Seezer was there to help you. Many times, he's told us the story of your journey together."

Bartleby didn't answer. Maybe Billy was right. Maybe he would never see his friend again. The ache moved up into his throat.

"I must go now," Billy said. He waved his powerful wings and began to rise.

"Wait!" Bartleby scrabbled back up on the edge of the fountain. "Will you tell Seezer we met? And that I wish him well?"

"*Quag-quog!* I don't think that's a good idea. If he finds out you're alive, but that you refuse to come, it might kill him."

The Perilous Plan

25

There were no turtle races at Chef Jerry's that night. Even though the boys and girls begged and wheedled, Bartleby refused to come up from the bottom. Lucky Gal tried to entertain the hatchlings by diving for crumbs. Bertha pitched in by doing her best tricks, which were Shake Hands, Roll Over, and Speak! But in a little while, the boys and girls trudged back to their tables with their heads drooping like wilted flowers.

When the garden was finally empty, Lucky swam down and nudged Bartleby's carapace. "I saved some bread crumbs for you."

Bartleby had never heard her voice sound so gentle. "I'm not hungry," he murmured without lifting his head off the stones.

"But you didn't eat any of the dinner Chef Jerry brought us. Without food, you'll become weak. Only a mighty turtle can survive the challenges of life in the bayou."

What challenges? Bartleby thought. I'm a pet in a fountain. But he only said, "I'm tired. Please leave me alone."

But Lucky Gal settled down right beside him. "I couldn't help overhearing what Billy told you this morning. You must go to Seezer right away."

"I can't."

"Why not?"

Bartleby heaved a sigh so deep it created a stream of bubbles. "It's too far. I'd probably get eaten by the Claw, the Paw, and the Jaw before I found it."

"*Phish!* You traveled a much greater distance to get here from New York. Seezer needs you."

Bartleby didn't answer. He pulled his head in. But Lucky Gal poked her snout under the front of his carapace. "Persistence is a good trait—but you are downright stubborn," she chided. "Tomorrow we must figure out a way for you to go. Good dreams, Bartleby."

But dreams were the problem. Bartleby's brain hurt from trying so hard to dream of a way Lucky could go with him to Seezer's gator hole. Yet nothing would come! Over and over, he kept seeing the same things—the sparkling water, Seezer and Grub on the mud bank, and the red streak. And each time he saw it, that streak became more terrifying. Was it fire? Blood? Bartleby was beginning to hate anything red, even though it was the color of his own ear patches.

When he was sure Lucky Gal was asleep, he paddled

up to the surface. The lights at the restaurant were off, but the moon lit up the fountain like a lantern. Bartleby swam to the place with the crack that looked like Seezer, and floated beside it. After a while, he felt more peaceful. His head and limbs began to grow heavy.

Pretty soon he saw Seezer turning round and round, digging his gator hole. He saw the alligator garfish rolling in the water, pretending to be a reptile. He saw Chef Jerry wearing his rubbery foot coverings and carrying his fishing branch across the riverbank.

He opened his eyes. Suddenly he understood what the red streak was. He just hoped it wasn't too late.

In the morning when Chef Jerry's truck clanked into the driveway, Bartleby swam to the surface. He'd seen the vehicle many times, but today he watched carefully as the man got out and opened the part of the truck that carried things. The back door dropped down so Chef Jerry could remove the crates of vegetables and other foods he'd brought to cook. Then the man lifted a basket of eggs out of a pile of straw in the truck bed. "Not one cracked," he commented as he surveyed them.

Lucky Gal paddled up behind Bartleby. "What are you watching?"

"My plan," Bartleby whispered. "The thing that will help us get to Friendship Hole."

For a long moment Lucky Gal was silent. Then she

drew her head up higher. "Good! I was hoping you'd decide to escape," she said finally. "But you know I can't go with you. You'll have to walk a great distance to find the woods. With my damaged web I'd slow you down—and there isn't any time to—"

"But we don't have to walk," Bartleby interrupted. "Look!"

Lucky peered over the fountain wall. "At what? All I can see is the red truck."

"That's how we're going to return to the riverbank," Bartleby said.

Lucky Gal stared at him as if he'd got gnats in his brain. "You may be clever, but no turtle can make a truck go."

"That's true, of course. But think, Lucky—how did you get here?"

"Chef Jerry caught me on the riverbank and brought me in the truck, but—"

"Don't you see? I came that way, too." Bartleby paddled around to face her. "Last night I realized something—humans must be creatures of habit just like other living things. If I'm right, then Chef Jerry must keep returning to the same fishing place. All we have to do is hide in the truck and wait for it to take us back to the riverbank. Then it's over the levee and into the woods—and we already know you can do that." Bartleby took a long, deep breath. "I think I can find the way to Friendship Hole from there."

Lucky Gal began treading the water so fast she was spinning in circles. "Let's go! What are we waiting for?"

"Hold on!" Bartleby reached out his webs to stop her. As gently as he could, he stroked her orange ear patches with his long nails. "It will be dangerous. Are you sure you want to go with me?"

"Of course. I'm still a bayou turtle at heart. Besides, I've gotten used to having you around. Without you this big bowl of turtle soup would be lonely."

Bartleby was happy, but he was also afraid. If something happened to Lucky, it would be his fault. He vowed to himself to be extra careful. "We'll know Chef Jerry is going when we see him put his fishing branch into the truck. But we'll have to figure out how to get inside it— and to get out of this fountain." Bartleby looked over the ledge and gulped. "It's a long way down."

"I have an idea." Lucky began splashing with all four webs. In an instant, Bertha came galloping across the garden. She lowered her big head over the fountain.

Lucky Gal paddled up to her. "Bertha, Bartleby and I need your help."

Yuh-yuh-yuh-yuh-yuh. Bertha wagged her tail.

"We have to go back to our home in the bayou," Bartleby explained. "It's very important."

Bertha's tail stopped wagging. She pulled back her head and barked. *Nuh-nuh-nuh-nuh-nuh!*

"Shhh, Bertha! Chef Jerry will think there's something wrong," Lucky whispered.

Mrrph, mrrph, mrrph, Bertha whined. It meant, "Something *is* wrong."

Bartleby paddled closer to the fountain wall and held on to the side. "Our alligator friend Seezer is very sick."

Grrrr, grrrr, Bertha growled. It meant, "I don't like alligators!"

"But this alligator is different," Bartleby tried to explain. "Once Seezer and I were a team—like you and Chef Jerry. Without him, I would never have known what home was."

Hrrrrr, hrrrruff! Bertha rumbled. It meant, "This is your home now."

"If I don't return to him soon, I'm afraid Seezer will die," Bartleby said. "I've got to go. Please understand."

The dog cocked her head, which was the way she looked when she was thinking.

Lucky Gal scrabbled up onto the ledge of the fountain and cuddled up to her. She poked her head under one of Bertha's earflaps and began whispering.

Bertha's eyes widened into deep, dark pools. *Arruff!* she barked. It meant, "Oookay! Tell me what you want me to do!"

Best Dog in the World

26

Bartleby heard the red truck rattle into the driveway. "Chef Jerry is here awfully early," he grumbled. "The sun isn't even up yet."

Lucky Gal poked her head out of her shell. "He always comes early on fishing days. Hurry, Bartleby, we've got to get ready for Bertha!"

Bartleby shivered as he stroked through the dark water beside Lucky. He'd been waiting for days. Yet now that Chef Jerry was finally going fishing, he felt sick inside. Unless the plan worked perfectly, he might not get to Friendship Hole. And even if he did make it, what would he find? Would Seezer be glad to see him? Or would he be too sick even to recognize Bartleby?

At the edge of the fountain, Bartleby and Lucky waited for Bertha.

"Maybe she didn't come with Chef Jerry today,"

Bartleby said. "Maybe she forgot about our plan—or changed her mind."

With a web, Lucky patted Bartleby's carapace. "Don't worry. Bertha is dependable and trustworthy. Besides, Chef Jerry never goes anywhere without her."

In the dim light, they watched the man go through the door to the restaurant kitchen. When he came out he was carrying his fishing branch, a large bucket, and a white box. He opened the door that was next to the driving wheel. Bartleby heard him shaking the jingly metal things he kept in his pocket. "Bertha, come on!" Chef Jerry shouted.

"Yes, Bertha. Where are you?" Bartleby called softly. He began splashing the water.

Suddenly, from around the side of the restaurant, a dark shape came bounding along. *Huff-huff-puff-puff,* Bertha panted over the side of the fountain. It meant, "Sorry I'm late—let's go!"

Lucky Gal nudged Bartleby. "You first," she whispered. "Good luck!"

Bartleby scrambled up onto the ledge of the fountain. Bertha stared at him. Out came her thick, pink tongue. *Slurp!* She licked Bartleby's carapace.

"I like you, too, Bertha," he grunted.

The dog opened her mouth. Her pointy, yellowish teeth came closer. Bartleby looked down her dark throat. He felt her hot breath.

"Bertha! Come on, you lazy gal!" Chef Jerry yelled.

Bartleby cringed as Bertha grabbed him in her jaws. To his surprise, it felt like being carried by something almost as soft as water. Bertha didn't use her teeth at all as she toted Bartleby toward the driveway. Her mouth felt as if it were lined with feathers.

When they got to the back of the truck, the dog's jaw tensed up. Her hold on Bartleby got firmer. Then she leaped. For an instant, dog and turtle were in the air before they landed in the back of the truck.

Bertha deposited Bartleby in the straw that was piled in a corner of the truck bed. Then she jumped off to go back for Lucky Gal.

"Just a minute, Bertha!" Chef Jerry grabbed the dog's red collar. "What's got into you this mornin'? You're runnin' around like a mother hen. You'd better sit up front with me." The man closed up the back of the truck. He led Bertha to the front and waited while she jumped in. Then he got in next to her and shut the door.

Vrrrooom! Chef Jerry gunned the engine.

"Wait! Wait!" Bartleby whispered. "Lucky, where are you?" He crawled out of the straw and pushed against the back door of the truck. "Help! Help!" he grunted.

The truck began to vibrate. Then it roared.

"Oh no, no, no!" Bartleby moaned as the truck began rolling down the crunchy gravel driveway. What had he done? Again and again, he tried to climb over the back door of the truck. But each time he came crashing down.

"Lucky, I never meant to go without you," he whispered. Sick with remorse, he pulled into his shell. It was hopeless. He was never going to see her again.

A series of earsplitting cries pierced his carapace. Then barks. Then long, bloodcurdling howls. Bartleby knew what those sounds meant. Bertha was grieving, too.

The truck rolled on. Bertha kept wailing. Bartleby could hear her nails clacking against the windows. Suddenly the truck jerked to a sharp halt. *Thunk!* Bartleby was flung against the back door.

Over the dog's ruckus, Bartleby could hear Chef Jerry shouting. "Bertha! What's the matter? You got to go?" Then came the creak of the truck door opening, and the sound of Bertha's paws pattering over the gravel.

Bartleby clawed up the rear door of the truck so he was standing on his hind legs. Just over the top, he caught a glimpse of Bertha running around the back of the restaurant. In a few moments she reappeared carrying Chef Jerry's tall, rubber foot coverings.

The man got out of the truck. "My waders! I almost forgot 'em," he exclaimed. "Bertha, you were worried I'd git snakebit, weren't you? You are the best dog in the world." He took the tall boots from the dog's mouth and patted her on the head. Then he pulled down the truck's back door. Bartleby had to scuttle under the straw to hide.

As Chef Jerry was putting his boots into the truck bed, Bertha leaped in, too.

"Come down from there," the man boomed. "You kin ride up front with me."

Bertha plopped down on top of the straw. Bartleby could feel her breathing hard.

"Come on now, Bertha," Chef Jerry said.

The dog laid her head on her front paws.

"All right, if that's what you want, then. You sure are actin' peculiar this mornin'." Once more, the man closed up the back flap.

When the truck started moving, Bartleby crawled out of the straw. "Oh Bertha, we've left Lucky Gal behind," he moaned. He placed a web on her big paw.

Bertha blinked her soft eyes at him. She took one of Chef Jerry's boots in her mouth and shook it gently. Out crawled Lucky Gal.

"Phew! That was close," Lucky said.

Yuh-yuh-yuh-yuh-yuh, Bertha agreed. She licked each turtle before she settled down for a nap.

Race to Friendship Hole

27

Inside the back of the truck, Bartleby's snout began to twitch. He took a big gulp of air. "I smell the Mighty Mississippi," he whispered. "We must be getting closer."

Yuh-yuh-yuh-yuh, Bertha agreed.

Soon enough, the truck rolled to a stop. Chef Jerry dropped the back door down and grabbed his fishing branch. He laughed as he removed the big, white box. "I hope the fish like the snails in puff pastry I've got in this cooler." Only Bertha knew the man's secret to catching fish—using scrumptious restaurant leftovers on his hook.

"Maybe I'll catch that gator gar this time, Bertha. I'll set up on that rocky ledge hangin' over the water." Chef Jerry toted his gear toward the river.

"Ready, Bertha!" Bartleby grunted as the man walked away. He turned to Lucky. "You go first this time." Bertha leaned down and opened her mouth. Lucky didn't hesitate or close her eyes before she stepped into the dog's jaws.

Bartleby kept his eyes on Chef Jerry. If he discovered that his "star athletes" were escaping, they'd be back at the fountain by the end of the day. But the man never turned around as Bertha jumped off the back of the truck— once! twice!—with a turtle in her mouth each time. Nor did he pay attention as Bertha trotted behind the turtles as they crossed the mud bank.

When they reached the safety of the tall grass, Bartleby stopped and looked up at the dog. He'd never expected her to become a friend, yet he was going to miss her. "It's time for us to part now, Bertha," he said. "I wish you could come with us, but Chef Jerry needs you."

The big dog lay down. Her ears drooped.

Lucky Gal pressed her snout into the dog's furry side. "Thank you for helping us. You've been a true friend. We'll never forget you."

"Bertha! Here, gal!" Chef Jerry yelled suddenly. "Where'd you git off to?"

Bertha stood up. *Mrrph, mrrph, mrrph,* she moaned softly. It meant, "Sad, sad good-bye." One more time, she licked each carapace. Then she ran back toward the river.

Bartleby and Lucky Gal scuttled over the broad levee. But by the time they reached the woods, Lucky was beginning to drag her bad web. She never complained, but Bartleby was worried. Even without an injured foot, he was exhausted.

"Perhaps we should rest in the pile of leaves under that oak tree," he suggested.

"All right—but only for a short while," Lucky agreed. "We mustn't linger too long."

Side by side, the two red-ears burrowed under the leaves. When they were settled in, Bartleby asked, "I've been wondering why Bertha decided to help us. Was it the thing you whispered to her?"

"Maybe," Lucky mumbled in a tired voice. "But let's talk later." She pulled into her shell.

Bartleby shut his eyes, but he couldn't nap. While he'd been planning their escape, he hadn't let himself think about whether Seezer was still alive. Now that he was going to find out, he was afraid. What if he was too late?

Lucky Gal seemed unable to rest much, either. Bartleby could hear her shifting on her webs. He felt her carapace moving beside his. "Are you awake?" he whispered.

"Yes. I guess I'm too excited to hold still. Let's move on!"

But getting through the woods was more difficult than Bartleby remembered. It seemed as if every bit of ground had sprouted crazily with shrubs, ferns, and grasses. Sometimes he and Lucky got tangled up in vines so tough, they had to bite their way through them. Or they had to climb over the great trunks of fallen trees that blocked their way. And they always had to be careful not to fall into the holes that lay hidden beneath piles of leaves and sticks. Who knew what creatures were waiting there?

In spite of how hard she tried to keep up, Lucky Gal began to trail farther and farther behind. When she disappeared from view, Bartleby climbed onto a rock to wait.

"Go on," Lucky called, poking her head around a clump of ferns. "I'll be all right."

But Bartleby wouldn't leave her. As she hobbled closer, he could see she was crawling on only three legs. Her injured web was tucked inside her shell.

"I need to stop here," Lucky said when she'd finally caught up. "You've got to continue without me."

Bartleby gazed around. "It's too dangerous."

"I haven't forgotten how to take care of myself," Lucky said, but she didn't sound angry. "Besides, a mother-to-be is the most persistent creature in the world."

Bartleby's heart leaped like a spring peeper. "A mother-to-be?" he repeated.

"Yes—we are going to have hatchlings."

"But—but why didn't you tell me before?"

"It's meant to be a secret for a mother turtle to keep."

"I'm going to have hatchlings!" Bartleby's webs were still touching the ground, but he felt as if he were flying. "What wonderful news! I'll wait here until—"

"No," Lucky said so firmly that Bartleby snapped his jaws shut. "To dig the nest and lay the eggs, I must be alone. There is no other way. That is why Bertha agreed to help us. She has a tender heart for hatchlings of all kinds."

Still, Bartleby was worried. It didn't seem right to leave Lucky alone in the woods. She could get lost. The Claw, the Paw, and the Jaw might be anywhere.

Suddenly Lucky gave his shell a hard push. "Have you forgotten you have a job to do as well? Seezer is waiting. Hurry to Friendship Hole! I'll find you there."

Reunion

28

The sun was nearly gone when Bartleby arrived at a small pond. He stopped and stared. The smooth oval reflected the trees and the sky like a perfect other world.

"Bartleby, I knew you'd return," a voice murmured. "Welcome to Friendship Pond. Seezer has been longing for you to see it."

Bartleby stretched out his neck and looked around. Behind a tree trunk he glimpsed a floppy brown ear. "Quickfoot, you're here!"

"Seezer invited us to stay in the hole he dug," someone called from the pond. It was Digger, floating on a branch with Baskin.

"Yes, he thought if we were all here, you would come back," Baskin added. "The basking is quite excellent."

"Seezer is a fine excavator and a fine friend—almost as good as me." With a splash, Big-Big sprang from the water onto the mud bank. "Hurry! Go down into his cave. Grub is there with him. He hasn't left Seezer's side."

"He asked me to protect the others. I'm in charge," Number Four called from the opposite bank. He whipped the ground with his tail and bellowed very convincingly.

Bartleby slipped into the gator hole and swam along the bottom. At the far end, he found Grub paddling back and forth before the entrance to a cave.

"Little bro'—glad you're back." With the tip of his tail, the skinny gator patted Bartleby's carapace. "Go on in. Seezer is too weak to open his eyes, but maybe he'll hear you. While you're with him, I'll go catch a snack. It's been a while since I've eaten."

Part of Bartleby wished he could hide in his shell, but he paddled swiftly past Grub into the long, underwater cave. On the muddy floor, flat on his belly, lay his friend. Seezer's eyes were shut. And when Bartleby stroked him on his snout, he didn't move. With trembling webs, the red-ear paddled up behind the alligator's right eye and whispered into his ear slit.

"Seezer, it's me. I'm here now. I'm sorry I stayed away so long. I was captured by a human, and it took me a while to figure out how to get back. But while I was gone, I learned something important. I was wrong when I said I didn't need you. I missed your friendship more than you will ever know."

Seezer didn't open his eyes, or nod, or grunt.

Never in his life had Bartleby felt more frightened. But he settled down on the alligator's head to wait for whatever happened next.

"Remember when we first came here, Seezer?" he murmured. "I didn't even know what a bayou was. If it wasn't for you, that smelly Old Stump would have swallowed me up. He was so much bigger and stronger, yet you risked your life to save me. But I was so awed by your courage that I never noticed the thing I should have admired more. I never thought about the disappointment you must have felt when you didn't find your family. You never despaired. You never gave up. You went on to—"

"Ssstop sssitting on my head."

Bartleby looked down. "You spoke!"

"I sssaid, get off my ssskull." Seezer's voice was slow and faint. "I need sssomething to eat."

"I'll go and catch you a fish. I'll be right back. Stay here!" Bartleby slipped off Seezer's head and began paddling toward the entrance of the cave.

It was dark when Bartleby popped up at the surface.

"How is he?" Billy asked. The egret was perched on the branch of a cypress tree. Plume was beside him, sitting on her nest.

"I heard you were back," she added. "Welcome."

"A fish! He asked for a fish!" Bartleby announced. He splashed the water with all four webs.

"I'll get it, little bro'," Grub called from the mud bank.

"I'd be happy to get it," Number Four volunteered.

"No, I'll get it," Big-Big croaked from a lily pad.

"Yes, one of you do it," Baskin grunted from his floating branch. "I'm going back to sleep."

"He asked me," Bartleby said. "I'll catch his fish."

Before he dove beneath the water, he cast a glance toward the woods. "Has anyone seen Lucky Gal?"

"Did she come with you?" Plume asked.

"Yes, but she stopped along the way. She should be here soon."

"In the morning, I can fly over the trees and look for her," Billy offered.

"No, she'll come on her own. You know how independent she is," Bartleby answered quickly. He knew Lucky wouldn't want to be spied upon. An anxious feeling fluttered inside him, but he reminded himself to be patient.

He stroked quietly along the bottom until he spotted a school of silvery minnows sleeping in a patch of water grass. He snapped up two and carried them carefully to Seezer. His friend's eyes were still closed. But when Bartleby slipped the fish between his long jaws, Seezer gulped them down.

Bartleby settled in next to Seezer. And once again, he began talking. He explained how he'd been tricked by the garfish, and saved at the last moment by Bertha. He described the fountain with the spouting fish, and his amazement at finding Lucky Gal. He told Seezer about Chef Jerry's delicious food, the crumb races, and the way Bertha had carried him in her mouth. He recounted the escape in the red truck, and how they'd almost left Lucky behind.

Seezer opened his eyes. "Where is ssshe now?"

"You're awake!"

"How could I sssleep with all your chattering?" With his snout, Seezer gave Bartleby the gentlest nudge.

Bartleby was overwhelmed with relief. More than anything, he wanted to share his secret with Seezer. He was sure Lucky Gal would understand. "I'll be quiet if you want. But I was going to reveal some news that I haven't told anyone else yet."

"A sssecret?" Seezer raised his head a bit.

"Yes! Lucky Gal and I will be having hatchlings soon. She is going to lay her eggs nearby so the young ones can grow up at Friendship Hole. We're hoping you'll help us protect them from the Claw, the Paw, and the Jaw— if it's not too much trouble."

"Sssweet Ssswampland!" Seezer's bellow was not much more than a croak. "Ssspunky little red-ears are just what we need. This water place has been ssso quiet, I've been bored out of my ssskin!" He lowered his head to the ground again.

"You look tired. I'd better let you rest now," Bartleby said. He was suddenly exhausted himself.

"Will you sssee Lucky Gal tomorrow?"

"I don't know," Bartleby admitted. "I left her in the woods yesterday. She insisted that she had to be alone."

"The woods are full of sssneaks and ssscoundrels—especially at night!"

"Yes—but I haven't forgotten the trouble I got in the last time I went snooping," Bartleby reminded him.

Seezer closed his eyes. "If I'd had a sssecond chance, I would never have sssent you away."

"I need sssunlight. I'm going to the sssurface."

Bartleby opened his eyes. He was surprised how long he'd slept. A tiny bit of daylight had already found its way into the cave. "Are you sure you're well enough?" he asked.

"To ssswim?" Seezer flicked his tail. "I'm sssure I'm ssstill ssspeedier than you." Bartleby followed him out of the cave and up toward the surface. But in spite of his boasts, Seezer wasn't nearly as fast or powerful as he used to be.

Quag-quog! Quag-quog! "Seezer's come out of his cave!" Billy announced as Seezer's head broke through the quiet water. He flew around the pond honking until all the creatures of Friendship Hole gathered on the mud bank.

"This calls for a celebration," Big-Big croaked. "We

should hold a swamp meet! We can have a croaking contest—"

"And plenty of eating, bro'." Grub smacked his jaws.

"Don't forget basking," Digger called from his log.

"Or storytelling," Number Four added.

The other creatures looked at him.

"I can tell how Bartleby outwitted four alligators in a race."

"Where is Lucky Gal?" Quickfoot's nose twitched as she tested the air.

Bartleby felt as if a cloud of gnats were beating their wings inside him. He'd been wondering the very same thing. "She got delayed a bit. But she should arrive soon."

Lucky Alone

29

Lucky Gal emerged from under a pine bough where she'd spent the night. Above her plastron she felt a slow, rhythmic pumping. It was as if her body were saying, *Time to lay eggs.* She stretched out her limbs and pressed her webs firmly on the ground. To her relief, her three-toed foot no longer hurt. Filled with excitement, she began hurrying through the woods.

After a while, her sensitive snout detected the scent of water. She opened her mouth and gulped the air to get more information. "There's a pond close by," she said to herself. "It must be Friendship Hole. But I've got to be nearer to lay my eggs. When they hatch, my babies must be able to reach the water quickly."

She trundled over rocks and under shrubs. The bittersweet smell of pond water grew stronger. When she got to a tree stump, Lucky Gal pulled herself up and looked around. Ahead in a clearing, she saw the shimmer of water. It was Friendship Hole—she felt sure of it. The pumping feeling inside her grew faster.

Cautiously, she crept to the edge of the woods. From there, a bank of tall grass rolled down to the pond. "Now to find the perfect spot for a nest," she murmured. She stopped and dug up a few scoops of dirt. It was loose and sandy beneath her webs. She turned around and dug a bit more.

"Hmmm, this seems just right," she mused. "But my eggs will also need sun to keep warm."

Lucky Gal looked up. Overhead the sky was bright. "Good. There are no branches to block the light from reaching my nest."

She squinted through the golden brown grass toward the pond. "From here, the path to the water is short and easy."

The pumping feeling grew so strong it made Lucky grunt. Suddenly she had to dig! Her rear webs began kicking up a shower of sandy soil. She excavated until the hole was about the same size as her plastron. Then she got in and laid eight eggs.

When she was done, Lucky crawled out of the nest and inspected her clutch. Though she could only see the round, tan shells, she imagined the bright little hatchlings that would develop inside. She might have gone on staring longer, but an anxious feeling told her they would be safer once she covered them up. Tired, but determined,

179

she began packing the earth back over the eggs. She worked until she'd made a secure and sturdy mound.

"I'll always be thinking of you," she whispered. "When you've grown strong and lively, I'll see you in the pond."

The afternoon sun was hot and bright as the alligators lined up on the mud bank to bask. Seezer and Grub left a space between them that was just the right size for Bartleby. On the other side of Grub, Number Four was stretched out, sighing as if he'd never been happier.

It was just what Bartleby had dreamed of when he'd been at Chef Jerry's. Yet he couldn't really enjoy it. "I'm a bit hungry. I'm going to dig for worms at the edge of the woods," he told the others. Trying not to appear hurried, he plodded across the bank until he reached the tall grass. There he stopped and clawed the dirt halfheartedly. He found a plump, sluggish worm and sucked it down his throat.

When he looked back, the alligators appeared to be napping. Quickly, Bartleby slipped into the grass. He'd waited as long as he could. He had to look for Lucky. He promised himself he wouldn't ask if he could help build the nest or peek at the eggs. All he wanted was a glimpse of her. If he could just see that she was safe, he'd go back to the pond again.

But as he pushed through the stiff grass, Bartleby detected an alarming scent. For a moment he stopped to sniff and gulp. His throat filled with the familiar reek of rotten breath and moldy hide. A powerful pulsing above his plastron warned him to turn back—but the need to find Lucky was even stronger. Bartleby plodded on ahead.

At the edge of the woods the stench grew stronger. Although Bartleby's webs wanted to hurry, he crept slowly and carefully through the undergrowth. If he snapped a twig, or shook a shrub, the noise could give him away. He wanted to see the beast before it saw him.

Whoosh, whoosh, whoosh, whoosh.

Bartleby ducked behind a tree.

"What a delicious surprise—a present on a present," said a voice that was deep and ominous.

At the mention of a "present," Bartleby's webs quaked. Still, he crept closer and hid under a bush that was dense with leaves. Cautiously, he peeked out. Face-to-face with Old Stump and his three guard gators, Lucky Gal stood her ground atop her neatly rounded mound.

"I love presents," crooned Number One.

"Tangy, chewy ones," agreed Number Two.

"And runny, drippy ones," added Number Three. He sank a claw into the mound that covered the nest.

"Back off! Those are Old Stump's presents." Old Stump snapped his tail across the guard gators' snouts. The three beasts cringed.

As he hunkered behind the bush, Bartleby tried to think what to do. He wanted to go for help, but he was afraid Lucky might not be there when he returned.

"I'm not a present, I'm a red-eared turtle—the toughest one you'll ever meet," Lucky Gal snapped. "If you eat me, I'll give you a stomachache you'll never forget!"

"Silly Present! Old Stump isn't going to eat you—unless you refuse to cooperate." The slimy giant flashed his snaggleteeth. "We only want to know where your water place is."

Bartleby was astonished. Even though Friendship Hole was right nearby, Old Stump couldn't smell the water! He reeked so strongly, he'd lost his sense of smell. It must have been the same for the guard gators, too.

"Cooperate with you? *Phish!* I've heard about you—and I know you can't be trusted. Besides, my water place dried up a long time ago." Lucky didn't budge from her nesting place.

"Lying Present—you can't fool Old Stump! Where there's a red-eared turtle, there's water nearby. Now lead the way before we become so thirsty we slurp down your eggs." Old Stump flicked his tail at the mound. It sliced through the mud like one of Chef Jerry's blades.

"Wait!" Lucky's head sagged. "I guess I have no choice. But you must promise to leave my eggs alone."

"Of course." The gruesome gator twitched his tail toward the guard gators. "Why eat a few puny eggs when there's a pond full of tasty presents waiting for Old Stump and his friends?"

The terrible trio wagged their tails like dogs.

"Hurry up!" With his snout, Old Stump pushed Lucky Gal off the mound. She rolled down the slope and landed upside down on her carapace.

"Heh-heh." Number One snickered at the sight of Lucky's ruined rear web. "Looks like someone's already had a nibble."

"Just a couple of toes. There's still plenty left," said Number Two.

"The tail looks like a tasty little bite," Number Three said.

As he watched Lucky Gal struggle, Bartleby could hardly breathe. If one of them tried to bite her, he would crawl out and chomp off its hind toe—no matter what happened afterward.

But using her webs and neck, Lucky flipped herself back up quickly. "All right, I'll take you there. But I warn you, the water place is far from here."

"Heh-heh-heh. If a three-toed turtle can get there, it should be no trouble for us," Number One said. He started slithering behind Lucky.

With a quick snap of his jaws, Old Stump bit his tail.

"Yeeow!" Number One yelped.

"Old Stump will follow the present. You three get behind," the putrid gator ordered.

Bartleby blinked. He couldn't believe his eyes. Lucky Gal was going the wrong way! She was leading them in the opposite direction. Without waiting another moment, he turned on his webs and scuttled back to Friendship Hole.

Bartleby's Posse

30

"As long as I'm alive, that ssstinking gator and his gang will never ssseize Friendship Hole from us," Seezer hissed. "I'll sssee to that!" He plunged his claws into the mud bank as if it were Old Stump's hide.

"I'll whip him, and rip him, and flip him if he puts just a toe in our water," Grub growled, waving his skinny tail in the air.

"Wh-why can't we just l-let him f-follow Lucky Gal away from h-here?" Number Four stuttered. "M-maybe they'll get lost for g-good."

"We can't leave Lucky alone with that backbiting bunch!" Bartleby exclaimed. "When they discover she's leading them the wrong way, they'll eat her."

"But there's four of them, and only three of us," Number Four moaned.

"I helped beat Old Stump once before, and I'll do it

again," Bartleby reminded him. "You don't have to be a bully to stand up against one."

"That's right!" Big-Big swam out from under a lily pad and leaped up onto the bank. "I'll kick those gators in the snout so hard they'll cry like hatchlings!"

"So will I."

Bartleby looked toward the tall grass and caught a glimpse of a floppy brown ear. "Are you sure, Quickfoot?"

"I owe Old Stump a boot in the snoot!" she answered.

"I might be able to tie up a tail—or a jaw," Curly offered from a branch overhead. The little green snake wound herself around and around the tree limb to demonstrate.

Quag-quog! Quag-quog! The egrets landed on the mud bank. "Plume and I will peck them till their hides are holey," Billy vowed.

"We must hurry before it's too late," Bartleby urged.

Seezer lowered his belly to the bank. "Ssscramble upon my back—we'll be much ssspeedier that way."

"Speed? You didn't say I'd have to move fast," someone said.

"Just try your best," another voice answered.

Bartleby glanced over his carapace. "Digger! Baskin!"

"We thought we might as well join you," Digger said.

"I can't get a moment's rest with this racket, anyway," Baskin grumbled.

Grub crouched down. "I'll carry you, Digger. And Number Four can take Baskin."

"Me?" Number Four swiveled his head and gaped. But he sank down in front of the crotchety old turtle.

"Try not to jiggle too much," Baskin ordered as he clambered aboard.

Like a caravan, the slithering, crawling, hopping creatures of Friendship Hole wound their way through the woods. Plume and Billy flew overhead, stopping in trees along the route. Many of the friends had never been more than a short distance from home before. To them, the towering trees and the vine-wrapped shrubs were unsettling.

Number Four twitched his tail. "We're getting awfully far from Friendship Hole."

"Yes, too far from water," Baskin agreed from atop his back.

"Are we lost, little bro'?" Grub called.

"I hate being lost," Number Four moaned.

"Does Lucky Gal plan to go on leading those gator goons forever?" Big-Big grumbled.

"Maybe we should go back," Number Four said.

At the head of the line, Bartleby was worried, too. He hadn't forgotten the last fight with Old Stump. He and Grub had helped, but Seezer had taken the brunt of the battle. He'd been the one who'd defeated Old Stump. But what would happen this time? There was so much at stake. And Seezer didn't have all his strength back yet. He needed more time to recover.

"Maybe you should lead them back to Friendship Hole," Bartleby whispered to Seezer. "I'll go on, and see if I can help Lucky Gal. Maybe I can distract Old Stump and the others while she sneaks away."

"Even if you did, we wouldn't be sssafe for long," Seezer replied. "They'll keep on ssseeking Friendship Hole until they find it. And they'll ssspoil our community—just like they did my old bayou. No, we must sssend them away for good."

Bartleby knew his friend was right. He was still afraid, of course. But Seezer's words made him feel more determined than ever.

"Do you know where Lucky is leading that sssmelly band?" Seezer asked.

Bartleby sniffed and gulped once more. *Could it be?* With the odor of Old Stump tainting the air, it was difficult to identify other scents. But he thought he detected something familiar—a mixture of fresh and ancient waters tinged with smells that were fishy and fumy.

"I think I do," he admitted. "If I'm right, it's a water place big enough to keep Old Stump and his gang busy for a long time. But it's also a place that has dangers of its own. We must ask our friends if they are willing to continue." He leaned close to Seezer's ear slit and whispered something.

"Sssweet Ssswampland, that gal is sssmart!" Seezer exclaimed in a hushed voice. "But you are right—no one's sssafety can be guaranteed. We may have to continue by oursssselves. You had better ask our sssupporters now."

Bartleby climbed down off Seezer's back and faced the group. "Friends—I have an idea where Lucky Gal is headed. It appears she is leading Old Stump and the others to the river."

"To the Mighty Mississippi, bro'?" Grub asked. "Ha! That water should be big enough for that greedy group of gators!"

"Yes. But it might take a battle to convince them to stay there. Old Stump is lazy. It would be easier for him to take over a home where the creatures are within easy reach of his jaws."

Big-Big hopped up and down. "Those gators have Lucky Gal. I'd like a chance to *convince* them to let her go!" He kicked the air with a strong web.

"You've never been to the Mighty Mississippi," Bartleby cautioned. "The bank of the river is a dangerous place. It's out in the open. Humans might turn up. Or dogs. Or otters. Even the creatures in the river sometimes emerge in search of an easy meal. There's no telling how this will come out. Some of you may want to turn back now."

None of the creatures said a word. Not a single one stepped out of line.

"Then we must ssspeed on!" Seezer bellowed. "We must help Lucky Gal before Old Ssstump needs a sssnack."

The River Helps Out

31

Old Stump emerged from the tall grass and saw the Mighty Mississippi. Without a word, he watched the vast, powerful river. His legs stiffened. His tail began to twitch. Suddenly he exploded with laughter.

"*Hargh, hargh, hargh!* You thought you could outsmart Old Stump!" His awful breath nearly knocked Lucky Gal out. "There was once another present who tried to trick the greatest gator of all. He would have become a snack if his friends hadn't saved him. But you don't have any friends here. *Hargh, hargh, hargh!*" With his long, thick tail, Old Stump smacked the mud bank. It missed Lucky's carapace by only the length of a minnow's tail.

"I thought you'd like this water place better than a gator hole," Lucky said. "The river is more than deep enough for your big gut. And you'd never run out of fish—not even you can eat every one in the Mighty Mississippi." But her voice no longer sounded as confident as it had in the woods. Her head sagged as if she were very tired. Her wounded rear foot was pulled into her shell.

"Old Stump doesn't want to live in a river!" came the thundering reply. "It's too much work. He'd have to swim in a strong current. He'd have to watch out for humans in boats. He'd have to chase his snacks." The big bully clamped a claw down over Lucky Gal's carapace. "Old Stump gave you a chance. He was nice to you. But you made him walk all this way for nothing! Well, now he's worked up an appetite. You will be his snack."

"I walked a long way, too. I'd like a little treat," Number One said.

"Yes. My stomach is feeling rather empty," Number Two added.

"All I want is a teeny-weeny bite," Number Three whispered. "I don't need much."

Old Stump smacked his jaws. "Of course. You may all go into the river and fish."

The terrible trio crept out on the flat stone ledge that hung over the river. Silently, they looked down at the thick brown water.

Number One shoved Number Two with his snout. "You go first."

Number Two pushed him back. "No, you!"

The two gators turned to Number Three. "I'm not diving in there," he said, backing away.

Old Stump ignored them. "Do you know what, Present? Old Stump is glad he waited to eat you. Red-ear is one of his favorite treats." He took his claw off Lucky Gal.

"You'd better look behind you," she said.

"Oh, no. Old Stump isn't falling for another one of your tricks." He opened his great jaws and caught Lucky between his teeth.

"It's no trick," said a voice behind him.

Old Stump whirled around. Shoulder to shoulder, Seezer, Grub, and Number Four faced him. Bartleby was on Seezer's back. The rest of the friends were gathered behind them.

"Let Lucky Gal go now!" Bartleby demanded.

Seezer clapped his jaws. "Or this time, I'll finish what I ssstarted."

Grub snapped his tail. "And I'll help, bro'."

"S-so will I." Number Four was shaking so hard, Bartleby thought he heard his teeth rattling.

"You dithering traitor!" Old Stump whipped his tail at Number Four. "You should be ashamed of yourself. Go join your brothers over there!" He flicked his tail toward the three guard gators that were hovering on the rocky ledge.

Still trembling, Number Four stepped forward. His tail dragged along the ground as he turned toward the rock where the others were waiting. Bartleby was disappointed in the cowardly gator, but he couldn't help feeling sorry for him, too.

As Number Four passed by the glowering Old Stump, he raised his yellow-tipped tail as if he were surrendering. *Crack!* Before the old giant guessed what was happening, Number Four snapped his tail across the great, smelly snout.

"Yeeeeooow!" Old Stump bellowed. As his jaws opened, Lucky Gal dropped onto the mud bank. Dragging her injured web, she scuttled out of reach.

"MY PRESENT!" Old Stump sprang toward Number Four. But before he could sink his jaws into the smaller gator's neck, Seezer leaped between them. Old Stump's teeth bit into Seezer's neck instead. Seezer bellowed and tried to pull away. But the giant gator had him pinned down.

At the sound of Seezer's shriek, Grub jumped on Old Stump's back and bit the gator's tough neck. "Hey, Four! C'mon, bro'!" he called.

Number Four leaped onto Old Stump's tail. The appendage was like a creature with a mind of its own. It battered Number Four's back. It bashed his skull. But Number Four kept his jaws tightly clenched on it.

Still Old Stump didn't let go of Seezer. Bartleby saw a stream of dark, red blood running down his friend's throat.

"Lucky! The outer toes on his hind feet are his tender spots. You take one and I'll take the other," Bartleby shouted. He scrambled around the back of the alligator and tried to latch onto the sensitive toe. Old Stump's nails clawed and stabbed at Bartleby. But the red-ear kept trying until he got a firm grip with his jaws. Then he chomped as hard as he could.

"YEEEOOOWWWW!" As Old Stump shrieked, his jaws opened and Seezer rolled free.

Bartleby and Lucky Gal kept on biting down. So did Grub and Number Four. With his webs, Big-Big began smacking the giant gator's snout. Quickfoot jumped on his head. Curly wrapped herself tightly around his neck. Plume and Billy dove down and pecked at his back. Digger and Baskin snapped at his belly.

"LET ME GOOOOOOOOOOOO!" Old Stump burst free and began running toward the river. Bellowing, honking, grunting, and croaking, the friends chased after him. When the terrible trio saw them coming, they dove into the water. Number Four gave Old Stump a last bite on the tail—and the reeking gator leaped in after them.

Splash! A great wave slopped over the bank. Below, the water foamed and churned. Then the river began rolling steadily once more.

"Welcome, Cousins," came a voice from the river. "Won't you come down to the bottom and help me eat the tender young crappie I've caught?"

True Home

32

Under a pink-and-purple sunset, the residents of Friendship Hole gathered on the mud bank. As he gazed at the quiet water, Bartleby felt a contentment he'd never experienced before. He was finally beginning to under-stand what it meant to be a real bayou turtle. Not that it was easy! Life here was full of challenge and danger. The creatures didn't always get along. But figuring out how to overcome problems and outsmart enemies made Bartleby happy to be alive.

"I want to thank you all for coming to my rescue," Lucky Gal said. "I thought I might not live to see my eggs hatch."

"Eggs!" Big-Big leaped up and down on the bank. "Where are they?"

"In a nest not too far away. We must try to keep the Claw, the Paw, and the Jaw far from here until they are hatched. Once the babies get to the pond, we'll be able to protect them."

"I sssuspect Old SSStump and his gang will ssstay away for a very long time," Seezer said. "His tender toes will be a sssore reminder of what will happen if he ever tries to sssteal our home away from us."

"How many eggs are there?" Curly asked.

"Eight."

"Harrumph! Only eight? A bullfrog mother can lay thousands at a time," Big-Big boasted.

"Yes, but eight won't crowd our pond. There will still be plenty of room for puffed-up creatures like you," Quickfoot said as she munched sweetgrass.

"Eight tiny turtles will be able to bask comfortably on my tail," Grub said.

"Or mine," Number Four added.

"They can sun with us on our log if they'd like," Digger offered.

"But only if they're quiet," Baskin grumbled.

"*Quag-quog! Quag-quog!* What will you call them?" Plume honked from the branch overhead.

Lucky Gal turned to Bartleby. "If it's all right with you, I've been thinking that we should let everyone help name them."

"Yes," Bartleby agreed. "You will all be their family."

Big-Big blew a huge bubble under his chin. "I think Little Big-Big is a very good name."